Goodbye, Darwin

Goodbye, Darwin

Edited by
Cavan Terrill & G.R.C. Lewis

Copyright © 2006 by Cavan Terrill and G.R.C. Lewis
Cover design by Jeremy Bowles.

Published by Apodis Publishing Inc.
www.apodispublishing.com

ISBN: 0-9738047-2-6

"At An Angle" originally appeared in *Aphelion*, November 2005.

"The Copy" originally appeared in *DawnSky*, July 2005.

Printed in the United States of America.

IN MEDIA RES PUBLICA

Trent Roman

It is perhaps cliché to say that science-fiction is one of the most flexible genres available to writers of fiction, and that its uses are multiple. Being set in the future, a science-fiction tale can be cautionary, employ its extrapolations as a warning. Being set in foreign places and times, a science-fiction tale can help us better understand ourselves and others by recontextualizing the issues of the modern world. The following tale does both, in a not-so-distant future, in a not-so-alien setting. The title of the story is a conjunction of two latin expressions: "in media res", in the middle of things, and "res publica", a public thing, from which the term "republic" is derived. And as the story opens, we find ourselves in a news room as a story breaks, following the action between two republics that were once one...

A story was breaking, and Jerry Timberland didn't have enough information to put it on the air. If there was anything that he found more frustrating, he couldn't think of it at the moment. He'd had the programmer pass along a quick note to Veronica Shelley at the anchor's desk, asking viewers to say tuned for late-breaking developments in Austin, but that sentence almost completely summed up their current state of knowledge. The note would no doubt reach the prompter shortly; at the moment, Veronica summarizing the latest economic reports on the growing trade deficit between the Republics.

Timberland watched his newsroom work, making calls, surfing through the Internet and competitor channels, trying to dredge up whatever details they could, trying to piece together a picture of what was happening. Almost nothing was coming through. None of the other channels had even mentioned Austin in their telecasts since they lost the link-up to Paul Bartling and his team; which meant that Direct News Channel could easily get the first scoop on whatever was happening out there – that is, if they could figure it out themselves.

He felt a familiar restlessness as he watched the others work. As one of the founders of the direct journalism school of thought, his natural tendency was and always had been to get right into the thick of things, on the ground and on the spot. He'd only accepted the post as content editor for the channel after it became clear that the leg wound he'd picked up out on the Ohio Crossing prevented him from being an effective field reporter; he simply couldn't move fast enough to catch some of the more recalcitrant interviewees, or away from danger should the need arise. It was hardly the first time he was behind the camera instead of in front of it, but he spent most of his time managing the staff rather than working on what went out to the feeds.

He could always go out on the floor and ride task directly, but that kind of micromanaging was a habit he was trying to lose. Veronica, who had become the crew's unofficial spokesperson since they had started sleeping together, had pointed out that it not only made the staff nervous to have the boss looking over their shoulder as they worked, it also communicated the impression that he didn't trust their skills. The latter was of particular concern to Timberland; when one embraced a reporting style as rapid as direct journalism, it didn't do to have employees who hesitated or were indecisive. Confidence was a must; apologies for inaccuracies could always be handed out later, but first claim to a story was ever a fleet-footed opportunity.

So instead of going down to the floor and standing over somebody's shoulder, he turned towards the large bank of monitors he'd had installed around his desk. The largest screen, right in front of him, was constantly attuned to an exterior feed on their live broadcast; whatever the audience saw was what he would see as well. To his right were four small TV sets, three of them tuned into their main competitors, one a direct feed from their own studio with no edits, showing at the moment only Veronica at her desk, minus the CGI background, superimposed images and digitized graphs that flashed across the main screen. The four to his left were multipurpose sets, each decked out with equipment for monitoring any given cable or satellite feed or for accessing pretty much any form of media storage device used in the last thirty years.

They were also wired to the DNC's mainframe, and Timberland used that access now to bring up Paul Bartling's last transmission. In accordance with the station's philosophy, the feed from Paul's satellite hook-up had been broadcast live even as the transmission was received. Paul had been doing a piece on the aftermath of the latest suicide bombing to hit the Austin area – this latest blast occurring after an almost two month lull in militant activity in and around the city, going off in a shopping mall and causing four deaths and thirteen injuries. Bartling's crew had been in Houston at the time, about to catch a plane back to Seattle, but changed their plans as soon as they saw the first reports on the Federated News Service.

Paul's handsome face appeared on the screen; behind him but still well within the frame, an ugly black scar on white faux-marble of a shopping mall floor, cordoned off with yellow police tape: "We're here in Austin, where the citizens of this peaceful community are still picking up the pieces after another tragic example of the violence that continues to plague the city." Timberland tuned out the words; coverage on these types of attacks tended to be similar, regardless of where they occurred or who was doing the reporting. Express dismay and sympathy, give the specifics, add historical and geographic context as needed, furnish a human element by doing interviews with the locals, and end the broadcast on a note of future caution, with a hint of potential tragedy.

In this case, Paul has gotten as far the context before the transmission cut out. Of course, most of their audience would already be familiar with the history of the city, given Austin's status as a bastion of Unionist thinking in the heartland of the Federation, but these explanations were a must. Timberland muttered the words along with his reporter; it was a familiar refrain: by the time the Two-State Solution was implemented, most adherents of liberal ideology in Federated territory had already moved to the Unified States, and vice-versa, seeking to live out the American dream in whichever of the Republics best suited their beliefs. But

4

the citizens of Austin, in a sterling display of Texan steadfastness, refused to abandon the state, abiding by the more restrictive laws of the Federated States without suffering the ideological shifts that places like Washington and New Orleans experienced, until the Local Rule Bill allowed the city council to effectively create a liberal oasis in the otherwise conservative desert.

Before Paul could launch into the chronology of rural/urban conflicts and the rise of the Evangelical militant movement however, the screen begins to white-out as though too much light was being directed into the camera, the sound gives way to a low roar like interference, before the feed terminates into the grayscale wasteland of static. Timberland had quickly changed the broadcast circuit back to the main anchor desk, where Veronica had gracefully advised viewers that they were having technical difficulties and would get back to Paul as soon as possible.

Problem was, Xue Ma, their resident tech-guru, had ruled out such a problem within minutes of the transmission being interrupted – unless the problem was at the source, with Bartling's camera crew themselves. A possibility, to be certain, but when Timberland had tried Paul's cell phone shortly afterwards, he'd merely received a recorded female voice telling him the line was currently out of service. He'd pulled up the numbers for the mobiles of Bartling's other crew members from the database, but with similar results. It looked almost as though something had crashed the entire local network.

Timberland watched the white-out three more times in under a minute before finally deciding that this situation justified a more hands-on approach. They needed to get something on-screen and soon, even if it was only supposition – they could always run a disclaimer right before giving out information. The point was that they would be able to say they were the first to take notice and track the situation. The fact that it was taking place in the Federated States made it all the more important; if they wanted to be taken seriously alongside the 'big three' network news stations, they had to demonstrate that their reach extended across the whole of North America. Only last month, Republic Reporting out of Los Angeles had out-scooped them with regards to the theft of nuclear material at Los Alamos, a major feather in the network's cap.

He walked down the short flight of stairs leading to his master station, leg brace clanking, making his way over to the feed operators. He asked them to start rolling commercials once Veronica had finished with her current article – a pre-game run-down on the International Football League finals. It was the Houston Gunslingers versus the New England Loyalists this year; a classic match-up with national pride on the line. One of Timberland's eventual hopes for his fledging station was the addition of a desk dedicated wholly to sports. Clapping his hands loudly, Timberland drew the attention of his newsroom crew.

"Everybody who isn't doing something critical related to the feed, I'd like to have your attention please." He waited as heads turned towards him. A number of workers in the back of the room rose from their seats and drifted closer, forming a wide semi-circle around him. "As you all know, something happened to Paul Bartling's team in Austin. Has anybody been able to find something?"

Heads were shaken.

"Nothing from the Associated Press or competitor stations," said Richard Elks.

"The Austin blogosphere is mute, chief," Jaya Rohatgi said from her station. Jaya had started calling him 'chief' shortly after he'd come onboard, and though he didn't much care for the title, he'd let it slide. Having already displaced their previous content editor when he took the post – who left in a huff to National News Centre – he wanted to get in good with the employees. "I'd think that whatever happened was either very localized or city-wide."

"Okay then, localized-effect first. Theories, supp-osition, random thoughts?"

6

"Could it have been another suicide bombing?" Richard ventured.

"Doesn't seem likely," Veronica said, joining them from the now-deserted anchor desk. Timberland was, as always, gladdened by her presence. In a career where so many people were little more than hollow shells wrapped around public images, Veronica Shelley was a woman of intelligence and compassion who never had to feign empathy or have her interviews ghost-written. "Two bombings in the same spot, within a day or each other? What would be the point? There's nobody there to kill except a handful of cops – and Paul's team."

"But don't criminals usually return to the scene of their crime?" Richard said in his defense. "I remember hearing that."

"Suicide bombers are generally exempt from that maxim," moribund Xue Ma answered, leaning against a partition, "due to the 'suicide' part of their job description."

Chastised and blushing, Richard suddenly decided that something on his screen was very interesting. Timberland resisted the impulse to shake his head. Xue could be a hardcase sometimes, but the boy really needed to grow thicker skin.

"What if Paul's team was the target?" Jaya put forward. "It's not as if your average Johnny Red particularly cares for the guy, the militants even less."

Timberland considered this. Bartling had attracted a fair number of enemies in the Federation ever since his award-winning exposé on the government's 'maternity wards', which Paul had re-named 'birthing chambers'. After revealing the almost prison-like conditions in which the Feds kept pregnant women who were considered at risk of trying to abort themselves or jump the border into the Unified States or Canada for the operation, Timberland and the network executives had had to fight tooth and nail just to let Bartling keep his Federated States reporter visa and security access. The government in Richmond had promised immediate reform, but the term 'birthing chamber' had already entered the public consciousness, particularly in the Unified States. Bartling was *persona non grata* for much of the FSA's government, but the Evangelical militant groups like Soldiers of Tribulation had gone a step further and called for his death. It was possible that one of those groups or their supporters had learned he was going to be in Austin and had the materiel in place to carry out the strike.

"It's a possibility," Timberland conceded. "Though I'd just as soon we come up with another explanation."

"Well, just a minute ago I was trying to get through to our contact list for Austin, and it seems like the city's telecommunications network is down entirely."

Timberland smiled at Jaya, grateful for the save. "Alright then, city-wide theories. What would cause us to lose contact with Austin? What would knock out the telecom network?"

"Nuclear explosion," offered Xue. "EM pulse fries anything electronic."

"That's not funny, Xue," Timberland reproached her. A number of people were quite worried about the break-in at Los Alamos and the missing plutonium; about the possibility of terrorists or militants walking around with a suitcase nuke. FSA Homeland Security had guaranteed the international community that the nuclear material had not left the country, but that was of relatively little comfort. "What could seriously cause a network crash?"

Xue shrugged, her kohl-lined eyes – the latest Seattle fad – revealing only her general annoyance at the world in general. "One of the nodes giving out and causing a cascade failure. A hack attack making incoming and outgoing signals rebound. Any number of things, really – the telecom network in the Federation is antiquated by any civilized standards."

"Maybe the FCRO decided to isolate the city," Veronica suggested, referring to the federal-level communications watchdog of the Federated States. The Federal Communications Regulatory Office had, in recent

8

years, taken to telecom isolation as a means of punishing areas frequently in violation of the Federation's decency standards.

"Might be," Timberland said, nodding his approval. "Jaya, the FCRO usually likes to flaunt their punishments. See if you can find something from them regarding Austin. Everybody else, back to work."

The sound of keystrokes and shuffling paper once again filled the newsroom as his crew turned back to their monitors. Timberland made his way back to his raised platform, an intern handing him a set of international briefs from the Associated Press on his way. Direct News Channel, still in its relative infancy, couldn't afford to maintain any offices overseas, and couldn't often send its reporters abroad. Instead, they'd settled for being the best as possible in North American coverage. Their signal went out to the entire Unified States, most of Canada and northern Mexico, with a new broadcast station even now being built to service the Prairie Provinces – and through them, into most of Montana and North Dakota. Their signal overlapped a great deal of territory belonging to the Federation, but the government there only had one official licensed network for news and wasn't about to sanction divergent views. Of course, citizens in those areas with a satellite hook-up could easily get their signal, should they ever care to tune in.

Timberland dropped the papers onto a rare empty spot on his desk, to be reviewed later. This was all old news, anyway – or old given the station's philosophy of instant-aneous news. That was the school of thought that he had developed in conjunction with Lester 'Lee' Littlefield: report what you know, as soon as you know it. Minimize editing and editorializing in delivering the news, but let the viewer see the staff's opinions afterwards. Get on the ground as often as possible, and use a lot of on-the-spot interviews with locals instead of quoting verbatim from government releases or consulting with experts. This produced a jerky, sometimes lurching style of news casting, but one which caught on quite rapidly with a population becoming increasingly concerned about media bias and disaffected with the glitz-and-glamour approach to journalism of Republic Reporting or the 'patriotic' slant of the Federated News Service. The more direct the broadcasting, the less time there was between the events themselves and the time it hit the screen, the more viscerally real and honest the reporting seemed. Of course, the flip side was an almost constant string of corrections, but then no system was perfect.

Timberland hoped that Bartling was, indeed, whole and hale. He knew Paul from a long way back, when the younger man had been field reporter for the National News Centre out of Boston. Paul had taken quite a significant cut in pay when he'd joined Lee and Timberland, but he had been inspired by what he thought would be a revolution in newscasting. The global effect was somewhat more limited, though imitator stations had cropped up in a number of countries, but Bartling was a true believer. Paul had been at Timberland's side when they had fought with the network executives to preserve their style of reporting when Direct News went from being a one-hour specialty show to a twelve-hour netlet. They had wanted a more conventional, less risky approach, but together they had prevailed in making the executives see that Direct News' different style was exactly what had made it so popular to begin with.

The familiar crescendo of music from the main screen announced the return from the commercial break. Veronica, smiling into the camera, welcomed viewers back then began rattling off the headlines, starting with an AP report on the latest developments in the civil war raging between the Baathists and the Koranists in the United Arab States. With a grace and genuine concern that Timberland had always admired, she worked her way through the items on her list, ending with a brief notice about increased tensions between Richmond and Portland over the Northern Crossing question.

She then leaned forward over her desk, lacing her fingers together, and, staring solemnly into the camera, said: "As far as this station has been able to determine, all outside contact with the city of Austin has been lost. The cause for this cessation of communications has yet to be ascertained, although viewers can be assured that we will be updating this story as it develops. In particular, the good will of everybody here at Direct News goes out to our long-time field reporter Paul Bartling and his team, currently incommunicado in Austin. And now over to the continental weather forecast with Sheila Dawson."

Timberland turned away from the screen, feeling particularly unconcerned about whether or not it would rain tomorrow. As much as he liked to think of himself as the cool reporter, the steel link between events and the public, Paul was a close friend and hearing his absence go out on the airwaves like that still caused a pang below his heart. Timberland knew perfectly well the dangers of being a reporter. It had never been the safest of jobs, and even domestic reporting had taken a more hazardous turn since the implementation of the Two-State Solutions – ironic, considering that the sundering of the old United States had been intended to reduce conflict.

His old friend Lee Littlefield hadn't lived to see his dreams of an entire network dedicated to their style of reporting become reality. He'd been killed during the Atlanta Riots, mistaken by the mob for one of the Neo-Segregationists that had been making life miserable for what minority groups still remained in the Federated States. This was before Richmond had passed the Local Rule Bill, of course, which, by devolving many federal jurisdictions down to the county and municipal level had, turned ethnic conflicts into occasional inter-community skirmishes instead of a string of intra-community uprisings. It had been Timberland's own exposé on African-American enclaves in Mississippi that had earned him his Pulitzer nod, the reception of which had been one of the critical factors in the network's decision to expand Direct News into its own channel.

And, of course, he had himself given blood to the cause, Timberland thought morosely as he looked at the steel cage that entrapped his right leg. As ill-luck would have it, he was actually returning from a job in Boston when his car ran over a homemade landmine that had been placed on the Ohio Crossing. The cession of a portion of northern Ohio to the Unified States so that its citizens would have a means of getting from New England to the Midwest Spike without leaving their country had deeply offended the nationalistic sensibilities of the more bellicose Federation 'patriots'. The relatively narrow span of the Crossing was ideal for militants targeting their former countrymen.

As a result, Timberland would always shake his head when he heard about this 'Northern Crossing' question. Portland wanted the Federated States to similarly cede a slice of territory from Idaho, Montana and North Dakota along the thirty-eighth parallel so that one could travel from Pacifica to the Midwest Spike without having to cut through Canada on the Transnational Highway or face the aggravation of Federated border crossings. Richmond was refusing, and Timberland thought it was a good move on their part. The Republics had enough trouble keeping the Ohio border secure; imagine trying to police a border running through most of the Midwest. Timberland had been lucky to escape only with a bum leg; if he had had a passenger that day, he or she would have been killed.

he phone on his desk rang, stirring him from his memories, two short bleeps indicating an internal line. He shoved some papers off the receptor and triggered the line. Jaya Rohatgi's bespectacled face appeared onscreen. "Yes, what is it?"

"Nothing about a punitive black-out for Austin on the FCRO's website."

"Damn. Alright, thank you, Jaya. Keep digging."

"Will do, chief."

Timberland turned towards the bank of monitors to his right. He still hadn't heard anything regarding Austin from their competitors, so that was a good thing as far as their exclusivity over the story was concerned. Of course, he hadn't been paying attention the whole time, but Richard Elks was monitoring those transmissions and would have called him if anything had come up. As he stared at the triple broadcasts, he felt that old sense of contempt for the 'big three' news channels resurgent. National News Center out of New England, slavishly adhering to outmoded concepts of impartial media that nobody believed in anyway. Better to be up-front about your biases and apologize later. Republic Reporting in LA, which had long ago forgotten the line between serious journalism and entertainment, dragging the entire profession through the mud with their lowest-common-denominator, anything-for-ratings approach.

And of course, the Federated News Service, headquartered in Atlanta. Although technically not subject to anything more than the FCRO's usual provisions against vulgarity, violence, sexuality and theologically inflammatory content, the good citizens of the Federation had made it clear that they wouldn't support with their TV sets any newscast they though was unpatriotic or overly critical of their government and way of life. Unable to sustain itself on the pittance of public funds earmarked for it by Richmond and thus depending entirely on its advertising revenues, the channel had become a joke in the media industry across the First World – but it also retained a massive share of the coveted North American market, so that laughter was often tinted with bitterness and resentment. Still, the fact that FNS usually waited to have the official line from Richmond before broadcasting most any current affairs stories meant that they were out-scooped by the other networks pretty much all the time. The Los Alamos break-in story was a perfect case in point.

Two short bleeps. Timberland pressed the accept button, and Richard appeared on the small inset screen. "Better come down here, chief. Jaya's on to something."

Not bothering to acknowledge, Timberland pushed himself out of his chair, feeling a slight twinge in his right leg as he did so. He made his way down the stairs as fast as his legs would allow him, his sights set on Jaya's workstation where a small crowd had already gathered, looking over her shoulder.

"What's happening?"

"Xue had the idea of calling somebody in the Department of Defense," Jaya began.

"He owed me favor," Xue added. "I figured if anybody had to know what was happening in the Federation at any given time, it was the DOD."

Timberland nodded his approval. The Two-State Solution had been designed to put into practice what was already reality: there were two clear ideological movements in the old United States, and the gap between them was only growing wider. With only one government, one nation, either nothing was getting done due to one side blocking the other or what was accomplished by one group was deeply resented by the other half. Despite this 'mutual break-up' between the more liberal and the more conservative factions of the old country, there had always been fears of civil (or international) war flaring up, given the results of the last attempt to sunder the United States. Though those fears had proven overblown, it was no secret that the military arms of both Republics kept a close eye on one another.

"I'd been hoping for some satellite access, but that was asking for too much given his rank," Xue continued. "He did, however, tell me that the DOD had been picking up increased activity on a number of military bandwidths around Austin."

"And…?"

"Xue's 'friend' gave her some numbers, and I'm accessing those bandwidths now," Jaya said.

"Wouldn't they be encrypted or something?"

"These transmissions are encrypted, yes, and there's no way I could hack my way past a military-level code. But a lot of the traffic we're picking up is actually transmissions being *re-broadcast*, and those original transmissions weren't encrypted. I've got a bead on a transmitted packet I think I can track to its source and access remotely from there."

As Jaya worked, Timberland saw streams of numbers and symbols race across the screen as a thick yellow line traced whatever information Jaya had latched onto back through the circuit diagram representation of the various Texan media storage facilities. Timberland looked towards the anchor desk and noted Veronica's current spiel, a feel-good story about collaborative medical efforts between the Republics on cancer research. It wasn't a story that hadn't been done half a dozen times already, so Timberland made a sharp cutting gesture at the feed operators and then motioned for Veronica to join them once she was done. He heard her starting wrap up her story in the background, but he'd already shifted his attention back to Jaya's screen.

"I've got a nugget," she said. "One of the original pieces of the data, no encryption. Quality's not the best, but it looks like it's got a number of graphic files in there. Let me see if I can't bring those up…"

Jaya entered a few more keystrokes and a new window flashed onto the screen, building up an image line by line. The first thing they saw was the sky, which had an odd reddish hue considering it was the middle of the afternoon down there. Then the top of the skyscrapers, the unmistakable cityscape of any major urban center. And between the highrises…

"Dear Christ."

Timberland wasn't sure who had spoken – it might have been him. He experienced the strangest feeling in the back of his mind, as though something particularly important was trying to get through, but keep bumping up against a barrier of neurons and synapses.

Xue Ma's voice drifted from his left: "I hate always being right."

Timberland felt a hand on his shoulder, the impeccably manicured fingernails clearly belonging to Veronica. "Is that what I think it is?" she asked.

Suddenly aware that everybody in the newsroom was looking at him, Timberland forced himself to really look at the screen and acknowledge what was there. Partially hidden amongst the heart of the skyscrapers although already eating away at their infrastructure, frozen in mid-bloom by a camera which had either survived the blast or sent out its payload before being hit by the accompanying electromagnetic pulse, was the unmistakable maroon shape of a mushroom cloud.

He felt an onrushing torrent of emotion at the sight of the picture beginning to cascade down through the pathways of his being, but quickly threw up a dam that was partly responsibility, partly conscious ignorance. This allowed him to begin analyzing again instead of merely reacting, the incisive reporter's brain making the connections and gauging the ramifications. The Los Alamos theft. Suitcase nuke – had to be, because of the amount of material stolen and because the explosion itself didn't look to be even half the size of the old shots of A-bombs going off in the desert or over Japan. It was still sufficient though to wipe out city block upon city block though, no doubt killing or poisoning most of the residents of Austin. The growing white light in the background, the rush of noise like interference; Paul must have been close when it went off. There was no hope for him now.

Timberland broke away from the screen and began giving orders. "Xue, I want to be able to break into all of our affiliates, regardless of what's on. Jaya, I want that picture ready to be splashed across every screen and website we have access to. Once that's done, keep digging in those files for any more images or information on the size of the blast. Richard, prepare a packet for the Associated Press – in five minutes, those phones are going to be ringing like the trumpets of the apocalypse. Make sure our name is on anything we send out – and Paul's, too. Veronica, anchor desk."

"What will I say?" she asked, voice tremulous.

"I'll write something out and send it directly to the teleprompter."

Timberland charged up the stairs to his station, leg brace squalling in unheeded protest. He dropped into his chair heavily, spinning it around to face the main monitor and began typing away, fingers pounding a furious rhythm on the keyboard.

When he looked up at the main monitor, Veronica was already back at her desk, absentmindedly brushing hair from her face. She picked up a pile of papers in front of her – probably just to have something to focus on – and stared into the camera. Her mascara had begun to run where tears streaked down her face. Timberland felt of moment of guilt that he hadn't noticed her crying before. Was she crying for Paul? Crying for all those people in Austin? Crying for a past that could not be recalled, or a future frightening in its uncertainty? All that and perhaps more, he thought.

"We interrupt your regularly scheduled broadcasting with this late-breaking, Direct News exclusive report," Veronica began, her gorge briefly rising. "From what evidence this station has been able to accumulate, parties unknown but believed to be affiliated with militant groups have managed to detonate a limited-yield nuclear weapon in the heart of Austin at approximately four thirty this afternoon."

The picture flashed across the screen in a rectangular box opposite Veronica's head, much larger than before and looking no less impressive for the visibly grainy quality of the shot. Timberland also noted that somebody had had the presence of mind to put up a scrolling bar at the bottom of the screen, repeating what information they knew even as Veronica spoke.

"We will have more information on this tragedy in just a few seconds, but first the team and management here at

Direct News would like to offer their most sincere and heartfelt grief to the citizens of Austin and all those who have lost loved ones today. Particularly close to those of us in the studio, we mourn the passing of award-winning journalist Paul Bartling and his team, in Austin at the time of the explosion and believed to have been caught in the blast radius. Though but one of countless victims of today's catastrophe, he will always be remembered as a professional dedicated to his craft and a good friend. He will be missed deeply."

A droplet of something wet fell onto his keyboard, and Timberland realized he was crying too.

RENEGADE

Matthew Bowron

I originally wrote Renegade as a school project, intended to show a person who hoped to find something in the city, and yet nothing turned out like it wanted to be. I also wanted to throw in the usual stories of treachery, romance, drugs and a bit of the sci-fi element to try to draw in different aspects of the audience.

Renegade: *n.* apostate, defector, deserter, turncoat.

I remember the city.

Neon dancing off black water; towers shimmering like diamonds.

Man-made of course.

I photographed it, studied it, analysed it.

But never visited it.

My parents wouldn't let me.

I used to scream at them, why?

All my other friends had, why shouldn't I?

I was eighteen.

I remember seeing my mother, her fists tightening with worry, her nurse's uniform bleached and spartan.

My dad standing there in his grey suit, arms folded.

Dunno what he does, lawyer or whatever.

We don't talk much, my parents and I.

Whenever we eat there's nothing said at the table.

They don't talk about their day or anything.

I know nearly nothing about them, besides the rules they lay down.

They had me signed up to be an Officer of Agriculture... somethin' like that.

I told them to stuff themselves, and I left.

I remember seeing you first at the station, beneath a magenta neon sign, eight-feet tall: BAYVIEW ARCHITECTURE UNLIMITED.

I had a rucksack with a change of clothes, a credit-disk and a book, 'Destiny Of The Stars' by Alex Thompson.

You wore a black dress with a silver crucifix on a long chain.

You noticed me before I noticed you.

You came forward.

You said your name was Lallie.

I told you I needed a place to stay.

You smiled, the magenta highlighting your smooth, tanned skin.

You led me towards a Magnetic Levitation Vehicle station.

I followed.

I didn't know what I was in for.

Screeeeeech.

The MLV-train doors opened. I stepped into the jungle.

Towering twisted spires of concrete and glass lined the abyss.

The platform elevated over fifty stories from the ground.

Upon the towers blazed massive screens advertising: Cola, Space Tours, God-knows-what-else.

The towers linked by thin bridges packed with people.

Gyrocopters swarmed like locusts, clumping together the further down you went.

I stood on the platform, gawking.

You grinned. " Welcome to Bayview."

"Pentax MB-12, Cray MCD player, Sony monitor, Compaq notepad reader... you sure he needs all this?" I asked, the list in my hand.

"*We'll* need it if we wanna keep our jobs."

You smiled, grabbing my arm, leading me to another electronics store.

It was day four.

You'd got me a job couriering packages for a guy named Alexis Thor.

I didn't understand what my parents had against the city.

All I needed was a friend like you, Lallie, to show me the ropes.

"So how you finding work?" asked Thor.

I was nervous.

His twin bodyguards stood silently beside him.

Thor's left fingers drumming, the right holding a lit Chent cigarette.

"You wanna smoke?"

"No… thankyou," I murmured.

Stacks of equipment were stored in the warehouse.

I didn't know how he could afford it all.

His Italian face lean, moustache and beard neatly trimmed.

He wore Armani clothes and Porsche sunglasses.

My reflection was thin and pale, hair dishevelled.

"Uhhhh… work is good," I stammered. " I'm g-grateful."

Thor smiled thinly. "Glad to hear it. You're a valuable commodity, mate. Just thought you'd like to know."

God, Lallie, you were amazing.

You laughed as you sat opposite me at the bar and sipped cherry-flavoured Hi-Lo-H2O. Mocha-chocolate eyes fluttering, golden curls bobbing as you leant forward, one knee bent. Dancers raved to techno-throb.

"So… in the burbs… you ever had a girlfriend?" you asked, smoothly.

"Uhhh… no," I admitted, blushing.

"Would you like one?"

I glanced down. " I…." You cupped my face and pressed your lips against mine. They were warm and moist.

The kiss stung, a memorial, as I sat in the police cruiser. A dozen questions burned inside as they asked a million more.

"They asked me all night! You say you didn't see them?!"

"No… I didn't," you murmured. It was the next morning.

"How did it happen?"

"They picked me up, as I was walking out of the alley, after you left."

"They just… picked you up?" you asked, blinking once.

"YES! You sure you couldn't see em?"

"No," you whispered. It had been raining. Thunder broke out in the distance.

You reached out and touched my bruise. I flinched.

"They asked about Thor," I said.

You drew back. "What did you say?"

"Nothing. Why did they ask, Lal?"

You frowned, eyes brimming. "I'm his niece and he tells me jack. How the hell should I know?"

You left me open-mouthed at the table.

I sat staring out the window, towards the burbs, another set of questions burning. One in particular: Why? Then there was a knock at the door of the apartment. I opened it. It was you, Lallie.

"Thor's a server."

"What the hell does that mean?" I grumbled.

"He sells black-tech to the ports and back."

I nodded solemnly. "How do I get out?"

You didn't look at me. "I told him you'd work for six months." You left, placing a package on my bedside table.

Christ, why didn't I listen to my parents?

Inside the package was a 0.357 magnum, microchip safety-lock, modelled to fit only my fingerprint.

I carried it under my flackjacket as I made the deliveries, always glancing over my shoulder whenever I heard a police siren wail.

There was also a pack of drugs. The sensation of pure bliss felt after a hit was called Eudemonia. A note attached, stated:

USE ONLY WHEN NECESSARY – LOVE LAL-LIE.

Took my first hit fifteen days later. I cried when it was over.

The drugs helped remove my depression, becoming an experience I fed into often.

Thor noticed a change in my mood.

Said I had a late night.

I'm getting nervous, Lallie. Nervous of what Thor's gonna do if he finds out I don't like being a crook.

I ran out of hits soon. Told you I needed more.

I'm an addict, Lallie.

And I need to get outta here, fast.

Took Steralin, to fight the cravings. Now I'm awake all night and can't think of anything else but Thor.

We were at the knife-fights.

I stared at the samosas in front of me.

"Not hungry, mate?" asked Thor as he chewed on his noodles.

You were seated beside Thor, looking at me with wide eyes, Lallie.

24

"N-not… really…. I g-guess." His bodyguards were silent. They didn't order.

"Well you better pull it together. We've got a dealership at Marydown in a few weeks. Some guy called Roefort. Need you to help me there."

That's when I realised. This was a loyalty test. If I wasn't there, Thor knew I was out.

Everybody has their demons, Lal. Now I had mine.

Received the instructions in the mail. Unmarked. No sender's address.

Meeting was Friday.

I had another letter with me. WITNESS PROTECTION (WP), Lal. I'd called anonymous and made them deliver a set of notes to the Post Office. Picked it up a week ago.

All I needed to survive were three things:
1) The location of Thor's operations.
2) His photograph
3) Evidence that would lead to his incarceration.

I needed you, Lallie. That's why I called.

You came that night, Lal.

Your hair was wet and you were exhausted, but you came.

We talked a little. Then I kissed you like I couldn't stop.

We lay in each other's arms, nothing but the crucifix around your neck separating us.

"We can't go on like this," you said, getting up and dressing.

"Why?"

"Just because," you murmured.

"Why, Lallie?" I repeated.

"Because we've got a big deal coming up. Thor doesn't want us to mix business and pleasure!" you yelled, dumping your bag down. "Roefort's dangerous… Thor's a good guy. He's trying to protect both of us."

"I don't trust him," I spat. You sighed, opened your mouth. I held up a hand to stop you from speaking further.

"Fine," you said, getting up and slamming the door behind you.

And then you left me. Again.

"Can't do it, Thor," I said. He signalled his body-guards to leave the room. You sat in the shadows, crosslegged.

"Why the hell not?" snapped Thor, smoke billowing from his nostrils.

"The cops, man! It's too dangerous!"

Thor held up a hand to silence me.

"Don't you think I know that? I know they talked to you," he said. "Didn't they?"

My eyes narrowed. "How do you know?"

Thor snorted loudly. "I have my informers," he said

I nodded, slowly, glancing at you for a moment, Lallie.

"You didn't say anything?"

I nodded again.

He grinned and slapped me on the back. "Figured. That's why I hired you, Mac, cause you're honest."

God I felt like killing him.

"Roefort originally planned to wipe out the cops," Thor told me. "Now says he wants to just blackmail 'em." The bar was noisy, crowded. "Me, on the other hand, I wanna nail 'em both. Roefort and the bloody cops.

"Roefort won't give me the virus easily. That's why I need his photo, to blackmail the bastard!" Thor slammed his fist on the tabletop. "And I want you to get it for me!"

I nodded. I knew what I had to do.

It was Sunday morning. Thor was at the coffee shop, near the gyro landing grill.

The meeting with Roefort had been arranged. Thor said how the enemy always lets his guard down for his friends. I used that info to my advantage as I sat on the rooftop with the high-powered lens.

You were at the arcade, Lal, drinking a milkshake. I waited as a jet-black gyro landed at the grill. Out stepped Roefort, tubby, white-haired, deep tan, dressed in flamingo-cream, hand extended to Thor.

Ten shots was all it took. I bolted.

I could've run forever, but I stopped at the printer's.

Stupid mistake. I'd waited until WP got the copies I left for them, before I handed the originals to Thor.

He was fuming.

I'd got his profile. I said there was no other way to do it or else Roefort would've seen the flash.

Thor said Roefort may know anyway, so we had to hit him tonight. I still have the mag, Lal. And I knew the look in your eyes as I nodded quietly, knowing either his life or mine ends tonight.

We all arrived at Marydown Docks at midnight, just as planned. I had a bad feeling. Too much Eudemonia and Steralin. My nerves were jumpin' all night.

No police evident, but I knew they were there. WP. Was Roefort? Had he prepared for an ambush? You had a shotgun hidden under your jacket as we got to the warehouse. Next thing I knew, a gun was pressed against my temple.

Roefort *had* planned an ambush.

"They say keep your friends close, but your enemies closer," said Roefort to Thor. Roefort's men armed, standing around us. He held up a vial. "I believe you are wanting this? Best biological warfare to wipe out the cops. And I'm gonna get a million," he turned to me, gesturing. "Thanks to your friend here."

Thor whipped out his gun. Everything moved in slow motion.

I saw you pulling out your shottie. I knew what had to be done. I fired four shots into Roefort. The vial dropped from his hand. You grabbed it, firing shots into his men.

Then the police came.

Thought Thor was gonna kill me, but he just grinned.

"Told you he was valuable," he said, pocketing the gun.

Cops explained you and Thor were working for them. How the goods I'd been couriering were just old stock, not hacking equipment.

They'd suspected Roefort for a long time.

That's why you needed me. Scared me into being frightened of Thor, not Roefort, so I could do the job. Get the evidence on Roefort that would lead to his capture.

"So that's why you chose me? But why me? Why not someone else?"

You smiled, Lal. "Cause that's the type of person you are. The type your parents raised." I gawked at her. "Your dad's a cop. Been one for years. Couldn't tell you about it… You've got a position too… if you want it." I said nothing as you reached out and held my hand in the rain.

I didn't take it. I'd had enough of the city to remember it for a long time. I still have my book and the crucifix you gave me.

I'll always remember you, Lallie, standing in your black dress, beneath the BAYVIEW ARCHITECTURE UNLIMITED sign, waving goodbye.

And thank you, for showing me,

I'm not a renegade.

WRITER'S BLOCK

Ali Al Saeed

It started with an image of old Moscow covered in snow. I wrote the opening scene and abandoned the story for months – as I often do – before finally coming back to it with a fully formed idea. The world I saw had a depression-era feel to it and I thought of turning writer's block from a state of mind, to an actual physical place. So the story became more analogical. I suppose I wanted, in a way, to vent my frustration on what the publishing world and writing life was becoming and felt that it would be served well as a sci-fi/spec-fic piece. It turned out later to be more about proscribed luck than passion or freedom.

"It is like a huge flea market, except you don't come to buy, you come to offer. What you have to offer is rarely desired" – Geffen Halloween, 2222, the year of the Sunken Auzielanda.

The street is long and wide, stretching to the void. Lots of bulky four to five storey buildings line both sides. There are a few taller ones but they all look the same. To the untrained eye, the road seems deserted. But it's not. There are wannabe writers and young authors and dying legends, all under camouflage. They hide behind unseen doors. They creep about on corners and in tight alleyways. They are everywhere and nowhere, and I am one of them.

It's cold. No, it's freezing. It's beyond freezing. The snow is falling effortlessly and the wind keeps picking up. I feel my insides shiver, my heart is like a turbo-mode vibrator.

I grip the thick blue e-folder under my left armpit, my arms crossed over my chest, squeezing myself to get some warmth. My feet feel as stiff and as heavy as bricks. I can feel my eyes almost hardening into crystal balls of ice. I can't feel my nose anymore.

I've waited my whole life for this moment. Everything I've done and been through has been to get to this point. This is when I will finally learn if my life has been worth living, or if it – at least what's left of it - will *ever* be.

The e-folder, this tiny, triangular touch-screen port-able computer that stores books in electronic form, which I'm protecting tightly under my now almost numb arm, is my original manuscript. The one I've been working on since I was twelve years old. It's my life. It's all I've got. It's all I've known and will ever know.

It tells the story of nobody and everybody. It takes place everywhere and nowhere. It's timeless. It's all and it's nothing.

It's about me and you and us and them, and the world and life and God and space, and feelings and actions and fate and destiny, and heaven and earth and death and tears, and all the things that ever cross the mind of every single human being on this planet.

I know that this book of mine, *Book of Mine*, is going to be hard to sell. I don't expect people to grasp it straight away. Any other book is just as hard to sell, and just as hard to publish, which makes things a little more difficult for me, for others. But everyone comes to this place with *hope*. All of us writers give our time, our effort, and we take all that we have within ourselves and we put it on paper, so to speak, and we retain the hope of finding someone who will appreciate that. In this day and age however, such app-reciation rarely happens.

It's a strange business indeed.

I finally arrive at the building, the same one as yesterday, Building Number 37. It is, on the outside, just like any building I've been to or seen; they are all faceless and featureless, without identity, without character.

Each day I wake up earlier than I did the day before, so I gain time for the increasingly sluggish journey. It's tough and exhausting, in this cold, walking the long trudge in the heavy, hindering snow, then standing in line hour upon hour in each of these buildings.

Once I've stopped walking, I begin to notice the movements around me. I can actually hear the noise of a complete city; car engines, footsteps, clattering and chattering. As I step ahead towards the buildings' tall and narrow doors, a man bursts out of them, cursing under his breath, teeth gritted and eyes wild with anger and despair. He stomps down the front steps then stands still, head down. I move closer to the doors. I hear a howling, crazy scream. Walking through the doors, I peak over my shoulder and witness a ream of e-papers flying and dancing through the air, and the man is on his hands and knees, weeping.

It happens. You see it all the time here, all around Writer's Block. Some give up, some go crazy, and some even kill themselves, or get themselves killed. It's a dangerous place, if you don't come prepared mentally.

This man in a heap at the foot of the steps, well, he is young. He obviously can't take it.

Me? I'm quite confident I'm doing it the right way. I've, as they say, done my homework. I've come here fully prepared. It's taken me 30 years to do so. Yes, there is a risk, there must be. But I'm here with the high hope that it's what *I've* got with me here that is *the* something that someone out there will want to read; some rich, fat bastard with all the time and money in the world to have the luxury of Old Reading. There's bound to be one of us succeeding in our quest, so why shouldn't it be *me*?

The last published book graced the world no fewer than two decades ago. Geffen Halloween, the man who came up with the Reverse Evolution theory, wrote it. He predicted that mankind will regress into *ape-kind*. According to his theory, we will start returning to our true origins in the next century or so; our legs will shorten and our arms lengthen, our bodies will become hairier and our whole stature will adapt to the nature of apes.

I couldn't read that book, though I desperately wanted to. I almost gave up most of my possessions to get my hands on a copy. It's expensive, you see, reading books, buying them. It has become the number one pastime of the rich, collecting, and sometimes actually *reading* books. They call it Old Read now.

Our planet started running out of trees, and therefore paper, soon after the twenty-third century. The Supreme Ruler of America, thank the heavens, drew up a Global Bill sometime during World War IV stating that cutting down a tree for any other purpose than a patriotic or a military act was a crime punishable by death. It still is.

Many rogue writers tried chopping down trees illegally, in their desperation to make proper old-fashioned, raw paper for their books. But they met their inevitable demise, poor souls, because the source of the paper used for the books was traceable and *they* knew who'd done it. It *is* a good thing, this ruling, what with our need for plants in order to breathe and all that. But then again, to those of us who truly breathe to write, it's difficult to adhere to the sensible way of thinking. Getting your book published, *on paper*, is like gaining the uncompromised certain knowledge that God is truly a man or a woman, or that he's any gender at all.

The rise of electronic books, and the fact that almost the entire human population is connected to the one network of computers and wires, helped ensure that published books are a thing of the past, and *any* interest in them now comes from the higher powers, from grand and rich men, and women, across the world. Now, *they* decide what is to be printed, whose book will be published, for *they* are the only people who can afford to obtain them and they are the only people who have the luxury of pampered time to indulge in them.

We, the authors and writers who are hanging onto our existence by threads, have only this place, Writer's Block, in a town with bleak and characterless buildings occupied by men with strange hats, in the old and forgotten part of the Dissolved Union of Great Europa, where one can see the Fallen Kremlin in the distant background.

Inside Building 37, as I wait alongside a considerable number of other hopeful writers for the elevator, the stillness of the atmosphere is stifling. I can barely still feel my limbs, my fingers and toes are slowly swelling as they begin to warm through and soften, reacting naturally to coming into the heat away from the onslaught of the freezing cold outside.

We clamber into the elevator, stacked against each other, shoulder to shoulder, our eyes darting left and right or up and down, avoiding anyone's gaze, concealing our e-folders under our overcoats. We each don't know, or don't want to know, who our companions are. We are each hoping we are harbouring that special gift, and each praying that we are *the one*, that what we've got is what will make history. Every one of us prudently wishes to be the next Halloween.

We spill out of the elevator in an automated fashion and stand in line. The concierge in the colourless waiting hall gives us each a number. Mine is 2222, which I think is a tad ominous. I look around me and there are only men, apart from the nice looking lady with wavy, red short hair and bright red glossy lips in the Process Office. Her eyes never steer away from her Typer.

I wonder for a fleeting moment how it would be if women were to write, just like men do. I've heard many stories about how women *used* to write in the old days, about how they were as good as men, if not even better, and I wonder if some of these men here today are holding their *wives'* books in the e-folders they are going to present. It is possible, but the Processors won't fail to see the ruse. They are more than adequate and accurate in their observations, the Processors.

Five hours of waiting pass and finally I hear my number called.

"Mr. Caterwaul?" the lovely redhead greets me as I step into the Process Office. "Please state your name, your proposed O.R. project and your P.I." Her voice is soft and low yet as crystal clear as pure diamond.

"I am Porter Caterwaul. My O.R. is entitled 'Book of Mine'. It is my first project. I come from across the Ocean. I am past my 40 mark." A silent prompt indicates for me to press my thumb onto the square machine, which will read my imprint, for final identification which allows me entry into the Commission.

There is only one chair, illuminated by a spotlight, at the heart of the big, black room. There is a wide screen in front of the chair, which is flanked either side by two long desks, barely visible in the semi-darkness. That is where the Processors sit.

The screen flickers. A familiar face appears on it. The image is in black and white. It is the face of an old man, a face that is blemished by black spots and imperfections. His thin hair is hanging from his scalp like cigar smoke, his eyes hide behind dark goggles. He is blind.

A booming faceless, slow, voice asks: "Do you know the name of this person?"

"Yes," I reply. "It is Writer-Master Geffen Halloween, the last man to have a paper-published O.R. book. His book, 'De-evolution of the Ape-kind', was printed in the year of the Regeneration of the Sun, 2202."

"Correct."

"Do you know what has become of him?" enquires a more feminine voice.

I hesitate.

"Thank you for your time Mr. Caterwaul," says the first voice. "You are dismissed." I stand up, feeling my anger rising. I did not even get a chance to speak of my book. But I mustn't argue with the Processors.

I lug my feet out of the room in silent desperation and frustration, more in myself than anything else. What *has* become of Mr. Halloween? How come no one has heard of him for so many years? My head is swarming with thoughts of him and of how I have blown another chance at reaching my dream and destiny.

As I make my way out of the office, redhead looks up at me and smiles and I think I see her mouth the word *sorry* to me, though this is probably nothing more than my imagination.

I enter the elevator and just as the shutters close I hear my number again.

"2222." I jump out of the elevator, barely fitting through the narrow slit of the doors I haven't given time to open fully, and I rush back to the office. The curious gazes of the other men follow me, alert and confused, and I even see the eye of jealousy.

"That is *my* number!" I exclaim, my heart pumping madly. "You have just called *my* number!"

"Wait a minute, please."

The lady gets up from behind her desk and whispers with the concierge for a moment. Then she walks into the black room. I am getting nervous and jittery, there is a bit of commotion coming from the crowds of writers outside. When she emerges from the room she has a wide smile on her face.

"The Commission of Processors call for your presence, Mr. Caterwaul," she informs me, indicating a hand towards the room.

I am in a daze. All that I can hear now is another faceless voice giving me instructions, "You are never to repeat what you have just been told." And I know that it isn't worth the risk of being included on the List, but in my head, it is there in my head...... *I am Porter Caterwaul, author of 'Book of Mine', and father to none. I am Porter Caterwaul, Writer-Master. I am Porter Caterwaul, the last man to have a published Old Read book.*

Luck.

I am only lucky.

I had almost forgotten that there is such a thing as luck.

Outside the snowflakes are falling more gently, settling on the ground, barely touching it.

There are strange faces passing by, some sad, some broken, some dead. I have fulfilled my destiny and dream but have failed to celebrate it. I can't.

Writer's Block seems to me now like a distant memory, a fantastical place heard of in ancient fables. My mind tells me it doesn't exist, my heart tells me otherwise. Stepping out of the building feels like stepping out of my life. What now? Do I go home and rest? Do I stay here, in this forsaken pitiful place where dreams and hopes don't matter, in this place empty of soul and spirit? Do I linger in the place where our literature is 'chosen' by luck, and for self-indulgence, rather than for its value or craftsmanship?

Now I understand why those rogue writers did what they did to the trees. All they wanted was the freedom to put their words and stories to paper so that people could read them and treasure the books.

I am confused and frustrated. I have lived my life for this book, to have it published, in this intolerable, industrialized, fastidious day and age. We've become a soulless, faceless world. Without the printed words in the books we can hold in our hands and read, we have nothing. And without the choice to do so, we are machines.

I feel the coldness piercing my skin, reaching my slow-beating heart as I make my way back to the hotel; my weary and heavy and damp feet leaving large prints on the blanket of snow. It is a long walk. Just past the e-library kiosk something draws my attention. I look to my right, towards a dark and filthy alley.

And there in the gloom, slumped against a pile of rubbish, I can make out the silhouette of a man. I move closer and stare.

I can't believe my own eyes. I must be dreaming. I look again, as close as I dare. I am *not* dreaming. It *is* the one and only, the great Writer-Master, none other than Geffen Halloween, rough and ragged and worn… eating a copy of his own book! I feel anger, but mostly I feel sick. I have always wanted to meet this great man. But to see him in this state is unimaginable. I gape at him. He is old and fragile and weak. He continues chewing on the paper of his book, ripping out one page at a time and sticking it into his mouth. He appears to be already half way through it.

"Mr. Halloween?" He ignores me. "You are *eating* your book, Mr. Halloween!"

"I am," he acknowledges, between chews. His dark goggles reflect my figure, even in the greyness of the ill-lit alley. "It is what I must do to survive."

"But Sir, you are a great man... you are a Writer-Master!"

"Nothing but two words," he mutters. "Here, have yourself a bite of man's fading history. It's rather tasty actually."

I take the piece he offers to me and hold it in my hand as if it is the most fragile, valuable thing in the universe. The feel of it is like touching a dream. Its surface is rough yet tender. I realize now that this old and crazy man is committing a grand crime and that I must report it to the authorities.

I have so many questions I want to ask him, so many that my brain is starting to swim in them. Just as I am about to speak, I hear the Vigilant Unit sirens howling, getting closer. My heart is racing and in spite of the freezing cold I feel heat all over my body.

"You ought to leave."

I do. I slip the half a page that the shadow of the man who is Halloween has given me into my pocket and I jog my way far from that alley. My head feels like exploding. I wish I had never come here. I wish I never had the curse of the ability to write. I wish I had a permanent writer's block and couldn't write a single word. But I don't. Will I meet the same fate as he did? Will I, one day far into the future, eat my own book, in a filthy, little alley of my own?

I throw my e-folder into a rubbish bin. It's not mine anymore. It's theirs. And I don't want anything to do with it, ever again. Seeing what I have just witnessed, and realizing the sleazy scheming of the O.R. Processors, I am no longer interested in being part of a superficial history.

I have made up my mind.

I will return home, over and across the Ocean, back to the great wide land where I have spent the best years of my life. I will return to my house on the little hill beside the lake and I will plant a tree. And I will tend it and nurture it as if it is my own child. And when it is ready, many days and months and years from now, I will chop it down and make paper from it. And on that paper I will write a new book with my own hand, and in that book I will tell the story of writing and of books and of Writer's Block and perhaps even the story of Geffen Halloween and that of Porter Caterwaul.

Then I will burn it.

PHAEDRA

Davin Ireland

Every writer's head is full of junk. Leftover words and images, stray thoughts, loose scraps of dialogue, anecdotes with nowhere to go. Sometimes these disparate strands come together in a way that is pleasing and we call them story. Other times they just hang around with nothing to do all day. For a long while, 'Phaedra' belonged firmly to the latter division, consisting of several stand-alone ideas that refused to play ball. And so there was this tale I'd once heard -- still not sure if I believe this one -- about a village in a remote part of Argentina where most of the population was descended from one man, an old ranchero prone to sleepwalking. Legend has it that, if you're down in that neck of the woods, you can still hear doors slamming in the dead of night as the latest generation of somnambulists drifts into the streets. Then there was the theory of Panspermia: the idea that life on Earth was seeded from space. What, I thought, if some of these spores were still out there somewhere, lurking in the far corners of the solar system? And what if some of them were sentient? Finally there was the very real menace of serious energy decline in our lifetimes, encapsulated in the horrible, gut-wrenching prospect of Peak Oil. The thing that brought all of these disparate elements together was, oddly enough, the music of Tangerine Dream, a German electronic band that saw its heyday in the 1970s. Ah, the '70s. I have always loved the music of that era, and it has often served as an inspiration for my writing. 'Phaedra', however, goes one better. It didn't just inspire the story, it is the story. Enjoy.

"It's a flat obsidian tablet," Belker explained as he hustled me through security, "about eight inches on a side, with a pale green impurity at the centre. That's all we know."

"Is NASA up to speed on this?"

Jim Belker shrugged, a gesture that could have meant anything. "The expedition was a joint effort," he explained, waving at an armed guard who gazed back in dour indifference. "Four teams rendezvoused at the Allan Hills ice field last summer, then went their separate ways. Maurice Pellagrin identified the stone midway through the second week. We've been doing the numbers ever since."

Jim stopped at an unassuming section of wall, swiped a plastic card through a slit in a console, and tapped in a key code. The unassuming section of wall slid back with a muted whoosh, and we were suddenly wandering unsupervised through the main viewing arena.

"To be honest, Serge," he admitted, "we were more or less done with the thing a couple of months ago. No markings, no discernible purpose, origin unclear. It was a washout, a busted flush. Aside from the fact that it was almost certainly of non-terrestrial design, there was very little to go on. Then the emissions started."

"Emissions?" I deliberately slowed the pace. "Nobody told me about any emissions. Listen, if this involves anything even remotely harmful, I want a Chemturion spacesuit and ultra-violet sterilisation right now or I walk, you got me?"

Jim scarcely broke his stride. "No need for any of that," he chided, "they're not *that* kind of emissions. I told you it's a stone, right?"

"Which makes it all the more unsettling."

This time Jim laughed out loud. "Look around you," he urged, indicating the tiers of plastic chairs that rose behind us, the glass wall overlooking the aggressively lit autopsy theatre, the used coffee cups littering a nearby side-table. "Do you see any biohazard precautions? Do you think I'd be standing here talking to you in a suit and tie if genuine danger were involved?"

I thought it over for a moment, realised Jim had a point. "I guess not," I said. "It's just that the scale of this place is..." I gestured at the surroundings, as if the word I sought might be plastered to the walls for my convenience.

"Imposing?" Jim cocked an eyebrow. "Don't let it worry you. Everybody experiences it the first time. When you're dealing with the securest item of real estate in the United Kingdom bar none, you need a while to adjust." He pointed at the ceiling and grinned, obviously relishing his role as impromptu tour guide. "This building consists of thirty-one stories, of which only five are above-ground. With the exception of the storage facility beneath us, you're as deep as you can go. Welcome to the belly of the beast, my friend. Practically speaking, a 747 could crash-land right on top of us and we'd barely notice."

"Some belly," I observed, peering over the glassed-in balcony. "Didn't think it would look like this, though." I regarded the gleaming tiled floor below, the pristine mortuary slab, the stainless steel trolleys of surgical instruments sheathed in transparent plastic drop cloths. There was even a rack of wall-mounted breathing masks attached to retractable tubes. Everything one might need to perform a genuine alien autopsy.

"Ever had occasion to use it?" I wondered out loud.

"I wish." Jim looked rueful and wistful all at once. "In budgetary terms, a bona fide little green man -- dead *or* alive -- would be just the shot in the arm the department needs right now. Instead, we're left with *that*."

He pointed at one corner of the marble slab. From this height, the object in question looked about the size and colour of a large cockroach. It was teardropped in shape, seemed to absorb most of the available light.

"Serge Napier," Jim intoned, face giving nothing away, "meet Phaedra."

"Phaedra? You named that thing after a character from Greek mythology?"

"Actually, no. But we'll get back to that. Right now I think I ought to answer your earlier question, the one about the emissions? We only call them that because the name doesn't readily suggest sentient life. In reality, we're talking about *trans*missions, Serge. Plain old audio signals."

"From *that*?"

"You got it."

I felt my skin prickle with all kinds of objections. "It's not transmitting into space, is it?"

"Nope. At least, not yet. For the time being, the signal's range describes a large oval that loops about six-and-a-half miles on an east-west axis, and is about fifteen hundred feet thick. Kind of like a misshapen doughnut, with this building right in the middle of the hole."

"Pretty spooky," I whispered, breath misting the glass partition. "Can we take a closer look?"

Jim shrugged. "It's what you're here for."

The most puzzling aspect of the project was the fact that Phaedra didn't appear to be doing any broadcasting of her own. The signal merely commenced a certain distance from the lab and ended some way further up. If it wasn't for the sheer coincidence of it, Jim informed me, as we descended a staircase concealed at the back of the main seating area, they may well have looked elsewhere for an explanation.

"Have you any idea why the transmission started when it did?"

"Thankfully that's something we *can* say with a degree of certainty." Jim performed his card-swipe trick again and hauled open a reinforced steel door. "Phaedra has been with us for about eighteen thousand years, give or take. She arrived here courtesy of a Martian meteor impact similar to the one that brought us ALH84001, although we don't believe it's from this solar system at all. Seeing as this is the first time such a signal has been detected, we believe something in the stone's circumstances must have changed enough to kick-start the transmission process. And we think we know what that change was."

As we approached the slab, Jim lifted two pairs of latex gloves from a wall-dispenser, handed me one, donned the other pair himself. Then he reached beneath a drop cloth on one of the steel trolleys and produced a glass jar with a screw-top lid. "See anything inside?"

I squinted through the curvature of the glass. "Doesn't seem to be anything there."

He shook the jar then dumped it back on the trolley. "You're not far wrong. Just before this whole escapade started, we found a couple of grains of pollen stuck to Phaedra's surface. That was the key. The ice field at Allan Hills is too cold to sustain complex life, as are the sterile conditions of the lab. Which is probably why this little lady," he said, giving the beetle-like shape a prod with his gloved finger, "was in some kind of suspended state for all that time."

"You mean cryosis?"

"Something like that. And she didn't have much luck after we moved her, either. A vacuum display case deep in a subterranean vault is nobody's idea of a thriving eco-system. Fortunately, some jackass left her on his desk late one summer evening, and hey presto, life intervenes."

"In the form of pollen."

"Uh-huh."

"From the ventilation system."

"Which caused her to awaken, as it were. And begin the scan."

I looked from my former employer to the strange object resting on the marble slab and back again. In all the years we'd been acquainted, Jim had never mentioned this building's existence, let alone his connection to it. I was beginning to understand why. "Unless I'm seriously mistaken," I posited, "you're telling me this is an extra-terrestrial probe sent here to root out of signs of life."

Jim answered in the affirmative. "We think Mars was its intended destination. Before it accidentally hitched a ride on that meteorite some eleven million years ago. Otherwise, yes, I'd say your analysis was spot on, Serge."

After taking a moment to digest this, I walked to the far corner of the theatre, where I leant my weight against a sink. All the signs indicated that Phaedra was an inert object -- a stone for want of a better word -- that contained no circuitry and no organic material whatsoever. As such, it was incapable of producing anything beyond the crudest vibration, and only then when struck with a large hammer. The notion of it transmitting *anything* was stretching the limits of credibility to breaking point. I didn't like it.

"In my estimation, this is a purely technical issue, Jim. I'm no use to you here. Hell, we're in the middle of nowhere as it is. If that thing detects a few trees and bugs, so be it. Why could you possibly want someone like me around?" Having said my piece, a tiny but vocal part of my ego absurdly hoped he'd come up with some corny line to justify my presence. *Because you're the best, Serge.* Like that. But he didn't. Instead, Jim Belker unsnapped his gloves, tossed them into a plastic pedal-bin, and told me that, unfortunately, we were looking at more than just trees and bugs.

"For the good people of Scattershot Rise," he explained, "life is about to change immeasurably. Over the past three weeks, give or take, they have unwittingly been putting the dough into the doughnut, so to speak. And now the time has come for us to go see the results."

"Courtesy of?"

"Black ops. We were testing a new generation of airborne surveillance equipment out in the deep woods when a set of onboard thermal imagers showed up something more than the dozen or so squaddies we were tracking as part of the exercise. I want you to see this thing for yourself."

"Will you be coming along for the ride?"

I expected Jim to pour scorn on the question, but all he did was eye me with something approaching pity. "My boss's boss said that if I let you out of my sight for longer than it takes to piss up a folded rope, I'm as fired as you are."

"Then thanks for the vote of confidence," I told him.

All this elicited from Jim was a weary roll of the eyes. "Look at this way, Serge. As a freelancer, you get paid a damn sight more than I do."

"Only because I'm dispensable."

There was no answer to that.

The village of Scattershot Rise did ample justice to its name, even in the dead of night. A series of low, undulating hills liberally sprinkled with barns and cottages surrounded a meandering High Street and a few neglected side alleys, all of it picked out by spectral, three-quarter moonlight.

Jim fleshed out the details of the location as I took in scenery through the greenish-grey haze of the nightscope. I didn't listen too closely at first. I was still acclimatising to the idea that a hunk of rock barely large enough to cover an open palm could successfully baffle the finest minds the British military had to offer. Stranger still -- and much harder to cope with -- was the presence of several ex-colleagues I had once counted as friends. They were spread out along the ridge at various strategic viewing points, and not one of them had so much as raised a hand to me. It was an unpleasant but inevitable consequence of my position. When Jim came out with that line about his boss's boss, he was talking about Lieutenant Mike Commerford, the guy who fired me. Can't say I blame the poor bastard. Not after what I did to him. It's just a damn shame no-one listened to my side of the story first.

"...broadcasting at subsonic level," muttered a voice beside me, "which required a booster small enough to fit onto the back of a microlight."

I lowered the nightscope and peered at Jim in the dark. After seeing the world submerged in ghostly green, plain old rustic night-time seemed as thick and impenetrable as a vat of crude oil. "Subsonic level?" I said. "How the hell can you record an audio signal nobody can hear?"

Jim looked incredulous. "With a booster, Serge, I just told you. And it's not a signal," he added, "not in the way you mean."

"Then what is it?"

Jim checked over his shoulder, fixed me with a humourless stare. "One word of this to anyone," he warned, "and I make you go away. Permanently. Understand?"

"Just tell me already."

Jim took a deep breath, and returned his attention to the village. "Music," he said.

"*Music?*" I dropped the nightscope into the dirt. "What the fuck is this, Jim," I hissed, "some giant piss-take? No, don't tell me: Commerford's devised a way of humiliating me that will give everybody a good laugh. Is that the brief, huh? Lead the homebreaker on a wild goose chase, then leave him tarred and feathered in a ditch at sunrise?"

"Cut it out, Serge." The order was firm but softly spoken.

When I refused, a meaty fist slammed into my testicles, doubling me over and putting me out of commission for the next twenty minutes. I had seen James Belker angry on a number of occasions, so I should have known what he was capable of; I just never assumed he would direct that anger at me. I was still nauseous and teary

47

when he resumed his story with the candour and restraint of a dignitary relaying an anecdote at a state banquet.

"It basically follows the form of an extended symphony," he said, "comprising three main movements and a shorter reprise section at the end. Much of it is atonal in quality and most of it isn't strictly what your average follower of the hit parade would call music at all. But our experts assure me that music it most definitely is. Considering fact that it combines the mathematical with the melodic, we shouldn't be too surprised."

"So what does it sound like," I mumbled, barely able to focus my eyes.

Jim searched for an answer as he peered through the nightscope. "Squalls of white noise, static washes, sequenced note progressions, other stuff I couldn't even begin to describe. And there are stylized audio effects, too. What sounds like the hissing of surf, the calling of gulls, even the playground cries of children. Come to think of it, that's what tipped us off."

"Tipped you off to what, exactly?" My growing sense of curiosity was acting as a slow palliative to the awful pain radiating from my crotch. Even my vision was beginning to clear.

"Come on, get up," Jim ordered, roughly hauling me to my feet, "I can't talk to you about this stuff around here." He half-led, half-dragged me along the slope and over the rise into the next dale before continuing his narrative. "You remember Hugh Wagstaff from R&D?"

"Sure," I said, recalling a face I hadn't thought about in years. "One of the lab coats. Bit of a loner, kept himself to himself. Great physicist, though."

"And one-time flower-child, too, would you believe? I never really liked him. Just a little too eager to cash in on his abilities once the hippie ethic died out. Nobody exchanges a commune for the establishment that quickly and retains any credibility in my eyes. But he was the best in his field, so what can you do?"

I allowed Jim to guide further me up a slope into a dense stand of trees before replying. "What did you do, exactly?"

"That one's easy. Brought him out of retirement along with a few of his contemporaries, just to see how he'd react. And you know what he said?" Barely able to conceal a smile, Jim shook his head, moonlight flickering off the planes of his face. "That he *recognised* it. He actually recognised the alien music."

I snorted in amusement. "Smoking too much home-grown in his old age?"

"That's what we thought at first. But he was so adamant, so steadfast in his conviction, that we were forced to give him the benefit of the doubt -- at least until it could be demonstrated otherwise. Serge, I'm going to ask you a question now, and I don't want you to laugh. Are you familiar with the name 'Tangerine Dream'?"

Tangerine Dream?

I thought about it for a while, drawing the fragrant night air deep into my lungs. The thicket wasn't as sprawling as some of the others we'd passed, but it contained a smattering of evergreens that lent it a nice, spring-fresh odour. I began to relax. Whatever was going on, this wasn't a practical joke: it was just too weird.

"Weren't they some electronic group from the seventies?"

Jim was already nodding, though the words that followed were not his own. "West German electronic group, actually," announced a figure emerging from the shadows, "and while I'd agree they produced the majority of their best work during the seventies, the band actually formed in sixty-seven." I glanced at Jim, suddenly found myself shaking the hand of a man who called himself Phil Javarro. Javarro looked as if he'd spent most of his life staring at a computer terminal, and was proud of the fact.

"Founding member Edgar Froese," he continued, releasing my hand, "a Salvador Dali protégé and promising

49

sculptor, who reputedly derived the band's name from Sergeant Pepper. Their first couple of albums were interesting but commercially weak. Then the band signed to Virgin Records in seventy-three, and so began their most successful period to date." He paused, either for breath or dramatic effect. "Their first effort for the new label proved a major breakthrough, both in terms of sales and critical acclaim."

"I still don't know where this is going," I told him.

Javarro exchanged a glance with Jim, who kept his face carefully neutral. "Then find the time to listen to this," he advised, and produced a cracked CD case from his jacket pocket. "This is the Tangerine Dream album Hugh Wagstaff claims he recognised upon listening to the unscrambled broadcast back at base. Keep it safe, and *don't* lose it."

"Great," I said, "what's it called?"

Jim waved his colleague back into the trees, and smiled indulgently. "I thought you would have guessed by now," he said. "This is *Phaedra*."

I wish I could have laughed. The moment deserved a great bray of derision and a hearty clap on the back. Instead, all I could muster was a mirthless grin. Jim wasn't joking. He meant every word. I guess I realised about then that my own unique set of skills might yet prove every bit as useless as I had first anticipated. I'm not a technician, strategist or military man of any description. But I do possess a rare talent. Psychic, witch doctor, medicine man, empathic, psyonic talent -- the labels come and go and they're all equally wide of the mark. Only the ability remains, and the gift itself is fairly straightforward. Simply put, I possess an innate talent to get inside other people's heads and see what they're thinking. To rifle through their mental drawers, as it were; to check under the rug for secrets. There's nothing supernatural about it. I just know where to look.

The trouble is, I went and used this wonderful gift on the wrong person. It was an anonymous contact, made through a mutual friend. We met in the next town under a shroud of pantomime secrecy. I should have guessed something wasn't right. She turned up drunk, used my appearance as a cue for an hysterical crying jag. Once off the gin and onto black coffee, I realised I'd heard her story plenty of times before. Middle-aged woman with a once-promising career, married to a career man who loses interest in her as the years roll by. There were affairs on both sides, naturally, only in this instance one of those affairs involved her own step son. Or at least, this is what the woman claimed. In reality, the whole thing was a ruse to gain a little husbandly attention. Clearly, she was mad. Unluckily, she also turned out to be Susan Commerford, Lieutenant Mike Commerford's wife -- and once back at base, the former opera singer blabbed every word of her false testimony to anyone willing to listen, liberally sprinkling it with references to that 'nice Mr Napier' and the advice I had offered. Now, that *did* get her husband's attention. It also got me fired faster than it took to answer the speaker-phone in my car.

But this is the thing. Commerford couldn't let well alone. As vain, dominant, and overbearing as he was, he knew damn well his wife was lying -- simply had to be -- yet that didn't prevent him from confronting his son with the unsavoury details of the story in a moment of bright paranoia. Naturally, Rick Commerford was incensed -- so incensed that an argument erupted, an argument so violent in its particulars that Commerford ended up banishing his son from the base, and his home, forever.

And all because I'd leant his deranged wife a professional shoulder to cry on.

As I pocketed the damaged CD case, and continued to breathe the soothing night air, it came to me that I knew the story from somewhere else. The names had changed, as had the locations and period in question. But the basic gist of it was otherwise uncomfortably similar to a tale from Greek mythology I had learned in school. The one about Theseus, his son Hippolytus, and a woman called Phaedra. In keeping with the particulars, Susan Commerford had even tried to hang herself -- though unlike her predecessor, the attempt had failed.

This was all falling into place with alarming neatness.

Trees and ridges, hedgerows and open fields, the closer we got to Scattershot Rise the less comfortable I felt. If our dating protocols were correct, the obsidian tablet back at the lab had arrived on Earth about eight thousand years before the end of the last Ice Age. Which meant the CD in my hip pocket constituted just about the oldest cover version in the universe. When I mentioned this to Jim, he merely snorted and clambered to the top of a ridge that had been mauled and sculpted by a mechanical digger to provide more comprehensive cover.

"Dali always claimed his moustaches were cosmic antennae designed to receive messages from outer space," he observed. "Maybe he wasn't kidding."

Together we peered over the lip of the ridge at the moon-drenched village. The peaceful vista scarcely registered on my mind. "You actually think Dali beamed one of these messages straight to his former protégé, who then made a *recording* of it? Don't you dare tell me that idea is being taken seriously upstairs."

"Not by me. But right now it's the closest thing we have to an explanation."

"No it's not, there's one much closer to home, and you know just what it is."

Jim kept his eyes on the High Street, Adam's apple bobbing uncomfortably as he swallowed. "Serge, I was hoping you wouldn't bring that up."

"What, the Phaedra thing? Don't you think the coincidence is just a little too obvious to be ignored?"

What Jim did or didn't think became less relevant in the following seconds, for out of nowhere there came a crash followed by the agitated barking of a dog. Then a man in a bathrobe and slippers staggered from a garden at the furthest edge of visibility.

"Here comes the first of them." Jim peered into the nightscope. "The broadcast must have started."

I was about to ask him why the two should be connected, when more doors crashed open and several gate-hinges squealed in unison. It looked as if the whole village had decided to come out and join the fun. I suggested it might be prudent to fall back a bit, just as a precaution.

"No need. The perimeter fencing'll keep us safe. Besides, it's not as if they're awake or anything."

The next few minutes demonstrated the unequivocal truth of that statement. Droves of sleepwalking villagers, some of them stark naked, others dressed only in strappy T-shirts and underwear, wandered in our direction. A hastily-erected chain-link fence at the bottom of the ridge curtailed their advance, but I couldn't help but feel trepidation at their inexorable, dull-eyed progress. Unable to go any further, the churning somnambulists suddenly halted, opening their mouths like baby chicks at feeding time, and crowded against the fence.

"Widening of the oral cavity improves hearing," Jim explained, checking the time on his watch.

"How come *we* can't hear anything?" I said. "Why isn't it affecting us?"

"Because we're awake, dummy. Now let's get going."

We walked the last thirty or forty yards down the slope to the chain-link divide and halted just out of reach.

Three taut lines of barbed wire strung at head height told me the Department wasn't taking any chances. "Merely a precaution," said Jim, "probably quite unnecessary given the circumstances." He checked his watch again. "Now listen to this."

Over the course of the next few minutes, the assembled villagers tipped their heads back and began to ... what, sing? Certainly, the sound they produced resembled song to an extent, but what I was hearing resembled something far more deliberate and functional. At best it echoed a simplified Tibetan chant, the entire group sustaining

53

a single note for whole minutes at a time. It was a remarkable achievement, and chilling enough to make the flesh creep.

"Do you think they're even aware of what's happening?" I murmured.

Jim shook his head. "You could stick pins in them and not get a reaction."

"How about tomorrow, when they're awake?"

"No different. We've sent moles through -- mock farm labourers, phoney tourists, you name it, they all draw a blank. Nobody seems to know what's going on. That's why we're trying something a little different tonight."

I watched as a straggler, a female form in a billowing nightdress, topped a low hill in the distance. She seemed to move with a lesser degree of assurance than her companions, and every now and again paused, as if uncertain of her bearings. But once Susan Commerford joined the melee on the other side of the fence, her piercing, classically-trained voice leant a greater note of urgency to the proceedings. I'd forgotten her early career as an opera singer. Now it served to focus the whole into a sharp, penetrating beam of sound that made my ears throb.

"An old friend of yours," said Jim. "We had her drugged and moved to an outlying farm at eleven this evening. That's why it took her longer to show up. Hear the difference."

When I refused to dignify the question with a response, he said: "We thought you'd be the ideal candidate to look her up in the morning."

"And what am I supposed to do," I demanded. "Ask her how she slept?"

"That's right. Find out what she remembers. And make sure it's the truth this time. I don't have the patience for another cock-and-bull story."

I was about to ask him if I had any choice in the matter, when a familiar voice reached us from further up the hill.

"Message from base," Phil Javarro practically squealed. He double-timed it down the slope waving a piece of paper as if it were a flag of surrender. He looked very excited. "It's started," he said breathlessly, pressing the faxed message into Jim's hand, "Phaedra's talking back!"

Jim swallowed, and for the barest ghost of a second his gaze angled at the star-prickled sky.

"Move out," he said. There was a distinct quaver in his voice.

"The thing that finally unlocked it for us," Hugh Wagstaff explained, "was a combination of data saturation-bombing and mathematical common sense."

We were gathered in the middle of a giant underground hallway which attached itself to the main body of the building by a tangle of subterranean rat-runs. All around us lurked the hulking forms of government supercomputers, the kind that don't officially exist; before us, sat the broken remains of Phaedra -- the enigma, silent and implacable on a glass table. As ever, Wagstaff was his monotonous and unassuming self.

"In layman's terms," he said, "we employed a souped-up version of the voice-conversion software used by the blind. Phaedra seems to have a penchant for audio, so we translated every line of text on the Internet into Morse code and bombarded her with it at super-accelerated speed. Slowed down it'd sound something like the clicking of a dolphin. At the rate we're broadcasting right now, all you get is a static hum."

Jim looked unimpressed. "Great. So plenty of noise went in. What came out?"

"Of Phaedra? Technically speaking, nothing. She's the same old hunk of rock she ever was. But in the next room our sensors began picking up looped bits of Morse in return, stuff recycled from our own broadcast and pasted together to form what you might call a loose narrative thread."

"How loose?"

Wagstaff looked like he couldn't decide if he was going weep, jump for joy, or excuse himself to the toilet.

"Panspermia," he said.

"Beg your pardon?"

"Panspermia. The theory's swung in and out of fashion for the last thirty years. Simply put, it postulates that all life on Earth was seeded from space." He looked at each of us in turn, watery brown eyes magnified by the thickness of his lenses. "I guess we can view this as a confirmation of the theory."

Still Jim was unmoved. "What else?"

"Evolution. Darwinian theory. That's not too much of a surprise. If the theory is sound, the same rules apply right throughout the universe. It's only beyond that point that things a little get weird. Phaedra skips most of modern science, doesn't even bother with Newton, Einstein, or Planck. Everything from relativity to quantum mechanics barely gets a look in. But once we get into the realm of obscure social scientific theory, *whoosh*."

Jim loosened his tie, obviously preparing himself for bad news. "Give it to me," he said. "Don't hold anything back."

I could tell he had been waiting for something like this.

"It starts with the seventh variable in the Drake Equation, the one that deals with the rise and duration of advanced civilisations. Phaedra's interpretation is rather involved, dependent largely on mathematical depletion models, and a number of theories previously thought beyond the Drake remit. X Waves, Kondratieff Cycles, Olduvai Slopes, stuff like that. The underlying principle seems to be that any planet with finite resources will evolve a range of species to exploit those resources, until, over time, said resources are exhausted. At which point the exploiters take a toboggan ride into extinction."

Jim's looked thoughtful. "Are we talking about any resources in particular?"

Wagstaff said that we were. "Which is where M. King Hubbert comes in. Hubbert was a respected geophysicist back in the fifties, a man who predicted that any finite resource, once reduced by half, would soon go into rapid decline. What made the theory so disturbing was the possibility that demand for such a resource might continue to rise regardless of dwindling supply, thus exacerbating the dilemma. He was talking specifically about oil, but I've seen the principle applied to just about everything from uranium powder to platinum."

Jim was starting to look markedly uneasy. "Go on," he said.

Wagstaff wiped a film of sweat from his brow, and frowned. "After trotting out Elliot, Kondratieff and Hubbert, Phaedra flagged up all the modern industrial fuel sources and their absolute reserves. Oil, gas, coal, uranium, methane hydrates, even helium three -- which is especially interesting because it's only available in quantity on the moon. These she added together to give what's known as our global URR, or Ultimate Recoverable Resources. All we get after that is a series of acute depletion graphs followed by drastically reduced population curves and numerous references to, um... The Book of Revelation."

"The Book of...shit."

"Oh, and a series of highly complex mathematical equations."

Jim's face was like thunder. "And have we solved those equations yet?"

"We didn't need to." Wagstaff allowed himself the merest hint of a smile, but it looked grimly out of place. "They were ours to begin with. Essentially, Phaedra left us a catalogue of orbital equations for the solar system and beyond."

"Conclusion."

"She's telling us the seventh variable in the Drake Equation is skewed. The ratio of advanced civilisations that destroy themselves through warfare, compared with those that survive, is secondary. Most of them run out of steam, quite literally it seems, before making it off their own planets. And if they can't do that, they can't harvest the natural resources of other worlds. That's why they fail to flourish. That's also why projects such as SETI are doomed to fail. No gas left in the tank."

"Christ. So it's this URR thing that's the deciding factor?"

"Ultimate Recoverable Resources, you got it."

I looked at Jim and Jim looked at me. The banks of computers lining the walls continued their doomed idiot hum. "So much for renewable energy, then."

Wagstaff seemed to agree with this, albeit reluctantly. "Wind power and switch grass might help you heat your home in winter," he observed, "but it won't take you to the stars."

I asked him what our next move was.

"Move? The stone shattered into a dozen pieces before you arrived. That's what the folks over at Scattershot Rise were for. Phaedra boosted their signal using our own equipment, raised it a semi-tone or two, and used the resulting sonic beam to compromise her own structural integrity.

"Like an opera singer and a wine glass," I added, finally connecting the dots.

"Which means no one will believe us." Jim ran his hands through his thinning hair.

"It also begs the question why." For the first time, Wagstaff had stopped looking smug, and appeared genuinely puzzled. "There may be thousands of Phaedra-like entities in the universe. Why go to all the trouble of travelling deep space for millions, perhaps evens billions, of years just to relay a once-only message in the hope it will be heard and understood at the first time of asking?"

"Beats me," Jim admitted. "Anybody care to offer an opinion?"

"Maybe it's a failsafe mechanism," I said. "After all, Phaedra didn't tell us anything new. She simply confronted us with a different perspective on our own knowledge, then left us to draw our own conclusions. A species wise enough to listen will take heed of such a thing and act accordingly. A race of morons will do the exact opposite."

There didn't seem to be anything to say after that. Jim picked up a shard of the broken stone and dropped it into his trouser pocket. "I think we have our answer," he said. "Drink anyone?"

We left the broken obsidian tablet lying on its marble slab and went upstairs for a nightcap. Outside, on the centre's rooftop bar, Jim and I tossed a few ideas back and forth. "Okay, consider this," I said. "Even before we knew what the stone was, it had identified Hugh Wagstaff as the man who could unlock its information core, and Susan Commerford as the means of its own destruction. The thing that linked them together -- the common thread, if you like, was an item of Greek mythology. Now, considering Phaedra couldn't read books, had never met either of the people in question, or ever encountered that bloody Tangerine Dream record, how on Earth did she manage to bring all of those disparate strands together? It's God-like in its conception, and so far-fetched I barely believe it now."

Jim shrugged and took another sip of brandy. "Maybe that's the best definition of the word 'alien' we have."

After mulling this over, I slumped back in my recliner and pondered the sweep of stars suspended above us in the clear night sky. I had never felt so small and limited in my humanity, and they had never seemed so majestic and so terribly, terribly far away.

"Maybe you're right," I said. "Maybe you are."

GOODBYE, DARWIN

Sam Kepfield

The tension between faith and reason is as old as man. Recent controversies regarding evolution and stem cell research, to name but a few, show us that the war between dogma and free inquiry is far from over. This entry shows what may lie in store for us when the battleground shifts from the physical sciences to the social sciences. . .

"I'm afraid that there appears to be some concern about your chances for tenure, Dr. Gunderson."

Henry Gunderson's heart sank. He was in his sixth year as an associate professor, and was up for tenure review this spring. Phrased diplomatically, in a soft voice, the department chairman's words meant that the academic career of Dr. Henry Gunderson, Ph.D., was effectively over, at least at this institution.

Gunderson looked at the dust motes swirling in the late summer sun blazing in through the large window in the chairman's office. He looked at the chairman, Dr. Willard McCall, noting the concern – not entirely genuine – on his doughy face. Then he looked at the almost sure cause of his looming academic demise, and tried to quell a rising bile in this throat.

It was a Friday afternoon. Firing on Fridays was a corporate practice borrowed by academia.

"Is it my teaching evaluations, perhaps?" As a low man on the totem pole, Gunderson taught two general survey U.S. government courses, with about 250 students each. He made students do essays rather than multiple-choice exams, to make them think about the materials. He didn't pass out B's for good attendance. Feathers were bound to be ruffled.

"No, your evaluations are above average, Henry."

"My publications? I admit that the article on arms control politics is behind schedule, but I plan on a trip to the Reagan Library this summer. Already have permission from the archivist."

"Er, it's, ah, publications, but not that one, exactly."

"Well, then, what exactly is it?" *Jesus H. Christ,* Gunderson fumed inwardly, *it's like pulling teeth with this guy.* McCall was a perfect administrator – never committal, never forward, hang back and see which way the wind blows . . .It had led to interminable faculty meeting, which Gunderson thought were a waste of time to begin with.

"Perhaps I could answer that, Dr. Gunderson," chimed in the third man in the office.

I'll just bet you could, you weasly little fuck, Gunderson thought. He detested everything about William Desjardins, the department liason to the Institutional Review Board. Desjardins was a short man with a stringy build. Under a perfect black helmet of hair was a face that was younger than its thirty years. The watery blue eyes, though, were those of a streetwise cop or KGB man that saw everything and forgot nothing, perpetually on the lookout for criminals or enemies of the state. His voice was tenor, but tended towards squeakiness when excited, which happened more than Gunderson thought decent. The accent was pure Alabama, no matter how much he might try to hide it; the accent also got worse with excitement. To top it off, he was always impeccably dressed, always dress slacks, oxford shirt and tie. Jeans, at least worn in public, were probably a sin. All in all, Desjardins looked exactly like the product of a little-known Arkansas bible college that he was.

"Yes?" Gunderson barely concealed his contempt for the man.

"We agree that your publications record is fairly impressive, Dr. Gunderson, at least in terms of volume of output, and variety."

"It should be." Gunderson had landed his first peer-review article while a college senior, and gone on to generate about three full-length articles per year. He had also, in the seven years since obtaining his Ph.D., written two books, edited two others, and co-edited another. Tenure should not have been a problem here.

"The concern is about the content of some of those articles."

Well, there it was. In retrospect, perhaps choosing post-World War II American poliitics as a field of specialization made this inevitable. People didn't tend to get excited about the politics of urban planning, or state legislative races. "Which ones, and what exactly are the concerns?"

"The board had some concerns about your piece in the *Wilson Quarterly*, Winter 2015, 'Prelude to War: Islamic response to American actions in the Middle East, 1979-2008.'"

"And the problem is?"

"We believe it takes an extreme anti-American view. Essentially, if you break it down, Dr. Gunderson, you're arguing that the United States deserved to be attacked on September 11, and again in the New Year's Eve attacks of 2007."

"Did you actually read the articles?"

"Well, I haven't read them in depth, but –"

"If you had, you'd realize that I set out U.S. policy in the region from the inception of the state of Israel down to the invasion of Syria. I concluded that based upon the statements of the attackers, that they were responding to our actions, and that this 'they hate us because we're free' line is a bunch of blind, self-serving, feel-good garbage. And I'm not the first one to make the argument, either. Read *Imperial Hubris*."

Desjardins was taken aback momentarily. Gunderson looked at McCall, whose florid face remained impassive. McCall wasn't going to lift a finger to help him, because he didn't have the backbone to do it. Easier to go along with the IRB.

"Your article in the *Kansas Law Review* last year, analyzing the PATRIOT Acts, with Professor Fan at the law school, also raised a few eyebrows." As well it should have – he and Fan had laid out the case that the PATRIOT Acts, I-IV, were the most shocking invasion of civil liberties since the Alien and Sedition Acts of 1798. Fan had covered the legal analysis, Gunderson the historical background. The Political Science Review had published it a year ago.

"Problem, is there?"

"Yes, well aside from the fact that Professor Fan is a naturalized citizen with suspected ties to the Chinese government, there was concern about the tone of the article. Particularly the closing paragraphs about encouraging civil disobedience."

"Those were mine." Gunderson said proudly. Hell, nothing left to lose now. Desjardins looked up from the file in his hands, and then lowered his eyes again.

"Your book, <u>Words of Faith, Politics of Power: The Rise of the GOP, 1980-2012</u>, published by the University Press of Kansas, here in Lawrence, last year, contains some material that the IRB felt was offensive to people of faith, and might violate some clauses of the University's EEOC policy, as well as its mission statement regarding non-discrimination. Frankly, a couple of the members expressed surprise that it had gotten past the editors."

"Really." He'd been raised a good Lutheran back in Minnesota, but somehow never felt included when talk turned to 'people of faith.' "Was it my tying the Republican Party to the Oklahoma City bombing to talk radio and the militia movement?"

Desjardins frowned at Gunderson's apparent good humor. "That was a problem, Doctor. They also had some questions about the validity of your research showing – allegedly – the use of racial images by the party."

"There's no 'allegedly' about it. You get a bunch of guys from the South who defect from a party because of civil rights legislation, and who run law and order ads fearutring a lot of black faces, and I'll show you a bunch of racists. Albeit fairly sophisticated, and more subtle than George Wallace or Bull Connor. I stand by that work."

"Which is the crux of the matter, Henry," McCall injected.

"Yes," Desjardins plowed in. "You see, the PAT-RIOT IV act and the Model Citizens Act of 2013 require that universities teach citizenship courses, and that they monitor suspicious activity which might tend to indicate some support for disloyal activities. And they are to report such activity immediately."

Gunderson's heart skipped a beat. "You're telling me that the University has turned me in to the Justice Department?"

"Oh, no, no. . .Not yet. Not yet, Dr. Gunderson." Those blue eyes turned cold and threatening.

Gunderson began to get it. "So what do I have to do to keep from getting reported, then?" But as he asked the question, he already knew the answer.

"We're recommending that you search for a tenured position elsewhere, Dr. Gunderson. We don't believe that the relationship between you and the University of Kansas is working out."

Gunderson nodded. McCall remembered another appointment, and Gunderson was ushered out of the office, past secretaries who cast their eyes down when he emerged. They knew. He was now officially a Pariah.

"Have a cigar," the burly bearded man told Gunderson.

"Smoking's illegal on the campus – hell, in this city," Gunderson protested.

"Well, what the fuck more can they do to you? It's a Monte Cristo. Enjoy." Gunderson accepted the cigar, bit off the tip, and took the preoffered light from Dr. Brian Dodge. He coughed a little as the smoke filled his mouth.

He hadn't known where else to go after the meeting with McCall and Desjardins. He had wandered down the hallway towards his office, head spinning, saw the sliver of light on underneath Dodge's door, and knocked. Catching Dodge in his office was a rarity, since he tended to avoid the Poli Sci Department, and hence the office politics and backbiting, as much as possible.

Tenured, with thirty years of teaching under his belt, one of the nation's foremost experts on Southern history and politics, author of twenty books and numerous articles, occasional guest on television and radio talk shows, Dodge was himself an institution. Dodge's crustiness, zero tolerance for bullshit, and profanity were legendary. Half a dozen department chairs had tolerated him and failed to change his ways.

Gunderson considered Dodge a mentor. Dodge's command of the English language was masterful. He possessed the ability to put pen to paper (literally – he abhorred mechanical devices of any kind, even typewriters) and turn out near-perfect prose the first draft. He was a demanding taskmaster, as Gunderson had discovered while collaborating with Dodge. Dodge was Master Kan to Gunderson's Kwai Chang Cane, Hannibal Lecter to his Clarice Starling. During their collaboration on four articles and co-editing the book *Coming of Age: The '60s generation in Congress from Freshmen to Leaders, 1970-2010,* Gunderson had come home swearing loudly. But he saw that Dodge had knowledge to offer, and he took it.

Gunderson related the details of the meeting to Dodge, who sat quietly puffing away with rapt interest. His size 13 boots were propped on the desk.

"'S a fuckin' shame, it really is." Dodge said when Gunderson was done, taking a long drag on the cigar, and blowing a cloud of smoke towards the industrial-strength air purifier beside his desk. "So that little fuck Desjardins was there, huh?"

"Yeah," Gunderson said, taking a small puff. "I tho-ught that here, of all places, I'd be free of this." Lawrence was easily the most liberal town in Kansas, and while not as progressive as San Francisco, it was an oasis of sorts in an otherwise conservative state.

"Christ, I came here thirty years ago to get away from the snake-handlin' Pentecostals. Looks like they finally done caught up with me." Dodge's speech tended to be less correct than his prose. Was it compensation? Or an indulgence? Gunderson never figured it out.

"You know, it's a sad state of affairs when you realize that twenty years ago, some hick from a barely-accredited Bible school —"

"—Correction. 'Christian college' is the preferred term."

"Whatever. That twenty years ago, his resume' would have been tossed in the trash with a laugh, and he'd never have gotten within a country mile of this place. But now, here we are, at a major land grant institution, a research university, and third-rate ayatollahs like Desjardins are not only hired, but taken seriously."

"You didn't grow up 'round these parts, did you?" Dodge asked rhetorically. Dodge's accent, from the hills of Kentucky, had been nearly erased from years in academia. It had been a hindrance when he'd been a young Ph.D. Today, a horrible Southern accent seemed to be a plus in some parts.

"Nope." Gunderson had been born and raised in St. Paul, Minnesota, University of Minnesota for undergrad, and Wisconsin for Master's and Ph.D. He'd left Minnesota for Kansas seven years ago. "Neither did you."

"Yeah, but I've been here long enough," Dodge chuckled. "And lately there ain't a whole helluva lot of difference," Dodge said with good humor. He was easily one of the most liberal members of the faculty himself. "I've been here going on thirty years now. And son, they do things different in Kansas these days. You can blame it all on Charles Darwin."

Gunderson search his memory. "The evolution mess? How does that lead to me getting fired?"

Back around the turn of the century, the Christian Right had been feeling their oats enough to begin taking on "liberal secular humanist orthodoxy." And evolution had been at the top of the list. It corrupted young minds, they said, by removing faith in God. It was all part of a plan that included removing prayer from schools, and not allowing the Ten Commandments to be posted. The Kansas Board of Education had removed evolution from its state standards in 1999, had put them back in two years later, but removed them again in 2005. The Big Bang theory had been next, written out of the standards three years later. The fundamentalists packed the Board of Regents next, and the agenda started over again with higher education. Kansas universities had fallen in the annual ratings ever since.

"And once they got a win on biological science," Dodge continued, "it was only a matter of time before they began feeling their oats and closing in on the social sciences. They shut down funding on psychological research. Anyone studying homosexuality from a source other than the Old Testament was driven off by poor evaluations or protests to the EEOC office, complaining of 'religious harassment.' And then it was any kind of sex research at ll. And from there it spread to sociology, history, and poli sci...And economics, too. Showing John Maynard Keynes' *General Theory* to one of them is like showing a cross to a vampire."

"And the goddamned administrators didn't have the guts to stand up to it?"

"Oh, fuck no. Sure, there was some opposition at first. But once it became clear that the Bible-thumpers were the wave of the future, they caved. Hell, they get millions in research money from the feds – you think they want to lose it? How on earth would they pay their faculty like Desjardins ten times more than he deserves? Any hints of secular humanism have to be stamped out viciously. And then they wonder why in the hell high-tech companies or biotech firms don't want to do business in this state. That means no partnerships with the university, and no potential to do ground-breaking research and get academic laurels heaped on oneself. So the best and brightest steer clear. And we get fourth-rate minds like Desjardins standing next in line for the chairmanship."

"You're kidding," Gunderson coughed. "Department chair?" The world truly had gone mad.

"Nope. Hell, why do you think he's the liason to the IRB? Gets to stick his nose all the way up the respective asses of the president and chancellor and provost on a weekly basis. He sure ain't getting there based on his rigorous academic credentials or his stellar research publications." Desjardins' 'specialty was international relations. His articles thus far read like press releases from the Bush or Frist Administrations, amounting to little more than apologia for the foreign policy misadventures of the last decade and a half.

"What am I going to tell Gabrielle?" Gunderson asked. His wife of five years had sacrificed to get him through his doctoral program. She had endured lonely days and nights while he took trip after trip to do research and to finish his dissertation, and had assured him that the finished product was not, in fact, a piece of shit fit only for burning. Gunderson felt like he'd let her down. And her parents, who had wanted her to marry her previous boyfriend, a law student who was now working on Capitol Hill as a Senate Committee counsel – they weren't going to let her overlook this for a minute.

Dodge rubbed his chin. "It's September now. You've got until the end of the year. I know a few people at other universities who might be looking for some talent. Check the *Chronicle of Higher Education*, and I'll do some calling around. I won't guarantee anything, mind you. Maybe just give you a few inside leads."

"That's good enough," Gunderson said gratefully.

Gabrielle took the news better than he expected. She had been raised mainline Methodist in Iowa. Her job as an

RN had brought her into contact with "faith-based" M.D.s more than once. She had seen prescriptions for contraceptives denied or destroyed by pharmacists, false information on birth control handed out by doctors, all in the name of "faith." After a physician had refused to perform an abortion on a woman with severe anemia, causing her death during premature delivery two months later, she had turned him into the State Medical Licensing Board – which had promptly found no fault. All it had accomplished was put her on a shit list at the hospital and passed over for promotion twice.

He told her after dinner, as they were both snuggled together on the couch in pajamas, she enjoying a glass of wine and he with a beer. No matter how much she said she loved him, Gunderson always felt that he was out of his league with her. Why would a blonde who looked like a Playmate and liked watching football pick him – a quiet academic type – for her mate?

"I'm sorry," he told her, his voice flat. "I really wanted to make it work here. I know you want a child, and we'd promised to wait until I got some security here. Now – Christ, I don't know if I can even get a job. Spend seven years here, tenure refused, that's not gonna look good to anyplace that's worth working at. The best I could hope for is some fucking community college in Montana. Or being a 'lecturer,' no job security, having to commute a hundred miles three times a week to two different jobs. Jesus." The words sank his black mood even deeper, and he threw his head back and stared at the ceiling of their apartment.

Gaby reached up and put her hand on his face, and cooed sympathetically. She'd heard his gripes about the department before. "It's not your fault, love. Desjardins is a little fascist, and McCall doesn't have the guts to stand up to him. So you can't trim your sails to suit them. Fine. I wouldn't love you as much if you did."

"Really?" He looked into her blue eyes, so warm and inviting, not the arctic cold of a gulag reflected in Desjardins'.

"Really. That's why I married you and not Rob. He was such a suck-up worm."

"That's why your parents loved him so much."

"Yeah, well for all his Godly posturing, I know a few things about him that would positively shock his boss." Rob now worked for Senator Tom Dailey, R-South Carolina, considered a hot presidential prospect for 2020.

"Like what?"

"Like he fools around on his wife."

"That's bad."

"With other men."

"That's – really bad. But at least he doesn't want to marry one, so the 29th Amendment remains inviolate."

Gaby laughed and took a sip of her wine. "We'll get through this. We were in worse shape when we first got married. Remember? Just work with Brian on a new position. I trust him."

He laughed. "Do I ever. Living in a studio apartment, futon on the floor, you working on your degree and me living off a stipend from the department. Christ, it's a wonder we made it. And your parents bringing up Rob every fucking chance they got." He took the large stone mug in his hand, and drank deeply of the ale. "Speaking of Rob, that gives me an idea. And no, you don't want to know."

The worries of tenure gone, albeit not in the way he expected, relieved his mind of worry. The next few months were a flurry of activity. He sent out resumes to colleges from Maine to Oregon, even one in Alaska – but none farther south than Kansas. He got a few replies, and some interviews which went well. By December, though, there were still no offers. Dodge had called some of his old colleagues from his student days, and others who had fled Kansas for other parts. He sounded encouraged by a couple, but nothing was definite yet. Gunderson was getting worried. He and Gaby began cutting back on their expenses, stashing away as much money as possible for moving expenses (best case) or groceries (worst case).

Academically, he now had nothing to lose, so he began outlining articles that he knew would curl Desjardins' toes. His lectures became bolder, questioning the official line and party orthodoxy. He even began criticizing the God Squad, as he now called them. It led to angry looks and protests from some, but he was past caring. His attitude was that if they were going to drive him out of here, he wasn't going to go quietly.

He attended a conference in San Francisco, which guaranteed sparse attendance from the faith-based crowd. In between presentations, he passed out resumes, made conn-ections, talked with a couple of Dodge's old cronies, and waited.

In the meantime, he also hunted up Kevin Murphy, a friend in the computer science department who had helped him set up some programs to analyze data for a couple articles. He had a simple request, which he was informed was probably illegal. But when told of the objective, Murphy gleefully told him it could be done by Friday, and no traces left. It was well worth the wait.

"It's an unusual offer, I admit," Dodge said. Gunderson was sitting in Dodge's cluttered office, looking at him through a haze of cigar smoke. "But one that deserves some serious thought."

"I know. I'm sorely tempted. But – moving that far? Jesus, Brian."

"It's not that far, goddamnit," Dodge said with mock exasperation. "Hell, it's closer to your old stomping grounds that Kansas is. The University of Toronto needs someone for an American studies program. Apparently they have a hell of a time figuring out why we Americans are doing the things we are."

"Yeah, no shit. I'm amazed we haven't invaded them. Again." The Canadians had been unsupportive of American

72

military actions in Iraq, Syria and Indonesia, and had raised hell about border security running roughshod over Canadian citizens crossing to the United States. The U.S. government had banned drug imports from Canada, a fact which some Canadian pharmaceutical firms did their best to skirt around, with the help of the Canadian government; the WTO was currently investigating that brouhaha. A half dozen other minor irritants – restrictions on beef because of mad cow disease, accusations of grain dumping by the Canadians, and farm subsidies – had all brought U.S. Canadian relations to their worst point since the War of 1812.

"Friend of mine from my doctoral days, Steve Lazzo, is on the faculty there. I sent him your c.v., and they're thrilled. It might ease some of the security concerns crossing the border."

"It's mine if I want it?"

"Yep. Might be able to find something for Gabrielle too, in their wonderful health care system"

"I'll think it over," Gunderson said. But it was the only concrete offer he'd had. He decided then and there to take it. Later that evening, Gabrielle agreed. He called Lazzo the next day, interviewed a week later, was offered a job two weeks later. He accepted without hesitation.

"I hate the thought that I'm running away," Gunderson growled, sitting in a chair at the airport. He and Gabrielle sat in a boarding gate at Kansas City International Airport looking out the window at the Air Canada Airbus 380 that would take them to Toronto. The setting sun gave the craft's hull an orange tint.

Classes would start in a week. He and Gaby had cleaned out the apartment, sold the cheap furniture left over from college, donated other items to the local Goodwill, and packed up the few precious or sentimental items shipping them to his parents' house in St. Paul, for temporary safekeeping. They were left with little but clothing and a large amount of cash, and a few leads on housing.

73

"You're not," Gaby reassured him. "You're being run out."

"Thanks," he said with a lopsided grin. "I feel so much better."

She kissed him. "It's the Bible-thumpers' loss if they run off their best talent. Leave them here to rot in their own mediocrity."

His sigh was lost in the roar of a takeoff. "I feel like a Jew leaving Germany in the '30s."

"You're being overly dramatic. No one's getting gassed."

"Not yet. You see the article on the AIDS quarantine camp proposal?" She nodded. A senator from Alabama had proposed, in response to the new strain of HIV emerging in New York and San Francisco, that those infected be identified and isolated in remote locations. Failure to do so in the early 1980s had led to millions of deaths, so the rationale went, but it could be excused in light of ignorance of the disease. Now, forty years later, with the disease a known risk not to do so was criminal negligence. The Senate Health and Human Services Committee would take up the proposal in a couple of weeks. The President was said to favor it.

"They didn't think Hitler would gas people either, until he started doing it. They're going to take the country back into the Middle Ages, undo centuries of scientific research and throw the First Amendment out the window. And they'll use modern law enforcement techniques to do it. In twenty years, America won't be any different than Spain during the Inquisition era, or England during the Reformation, where being the wrong religion could get you thrown in a dungeon, or tortured until you died or converted.

"So what was all the hubbub with Desjardins just before the semester ended?" Gaby asked, changing the subject.

Gunderson chuckled. "Seems that Mr. Desjardins was given to viewing unapproved sites on the internet from his office computer."

"I'm not surprised," Gaby said archly. "You saw his wife." Harmony Desjardins, meek, submissive and mousy, was a perfect fit for her husband. Gaby's face lit up. "You didn't –"

"No, no," Gunderson waved his hands. "Didn't need to. I – let's just call it a hunch, and thank your ex-boyfriend Rob."

"One down," Gaby said brightly.

"Yeah. And how many more to go? That's someone else's job. I'm done here," he said, as the intercom announced their flight, and they stood to board the plane.

An hour later, Henry Gunderson watched the ground recede beneath him as the jet lumbered into the air. While Gaby read a paperback bought at the terminal, Gunderson stared out the window, accepting the fact of his semi-exile, as night fell on Kansas.

REQUIEM FOR A RUNNER

Gwendolyn Perkins

When I was younger, I used to be fascinated by black and white movies, particularly the hardboiled genre. Something about the gritty aura of blacks and greys against the soft tones of the humans within always appealed to me- it reminds me of the port city which I call home. While this fascination with noir eventually blended with a love of science fiction, it didn't entirely fade and this is where "Requiem for a Runner" found its first origins.

For me, this is a story of vertical stratification. Like an old movie, the rich live in tall skyscrapers that replace the ivory towers of fantasy fiction. The poor are left to the streets, to scrabble their lives out as best they can in the shadows of those buildings, both literal and metaphorical. The protagonist, Diego, is one of those left on the streets- while his profession gives him passage to that upper level, it is not a world to which he belongs.

I invite you to read the following story and decide for yourself whether these confines exist in our own society. Is this a world that could come to pass? I believe so...

She's already screaming before I open the door.

"Calm down," I say, knuckles white on the handle of my kit as I shut the door behind me. No sense in bringing the neighbors down on us as well. "Where is he?" All I get from her is sharp breathing in and out as she either readies for a wail or tries to stop herself. I don't have time to figure out which is which.

I step into the living room. He's on the floor in front of me, a dark shape on dirty ground. I can't see anything. They've got the lights turned off and the only window in the place is a small square not far above street level.

"You." To the girl. She's finally managed to bring the wail to a whimper. "How long?"

"I-"

"How long has he been out?"

"I dunno- a minute, maybe?" A minute. That could be three. It could be four. Six minutes is when a brain starts to die.

No time.

I reach down, reach out for a hand, call to her to light a candle, get a lamp, whatever. I have to see this. The hand I touch is wet, blood on the fingers. An aneurysm? No, something worse.

"I've got a do-it-yourselfer here." My words spit into the radio and I know they're starting to panic on the other

77

end. This is not what I'm here for. I'm here to fix a game machine. Nothing more.

My fingers fumble with the kit, opening it and pulling out a meter. I gently feel around the guy's head. The hair is snarled, greasy- he's obviously not bathed in a while. It takes a minute to find the jack and when I do, it's slick with blood from where someone's taken a screwdriver maybe. Tried to pry it out or tighten it. I could kill her.

The best I can do is wipe it off and pray.

At that moment, the world slows.

It's a difficult sort of feeling to explain, the sudden clarity that comes when you only have one chance to get it right. Sixty seconds can become a year in a breath. The girl is standing there, breathing hard in the shadow, her legs illuminated every couple of seconds by the flash of the television on the floor. Her left knee's scabbed. Her foot scuffs a pile of CDs, each one written on with a thick black marker, and then stops, shuffling in front protectively as she notices my eyes turn.

"Your name."

"My name?" She asks.

"We don't have time for this." I say. "Turn on the light. Tell me what happened." Then I raise the radio, coughing the words out. "I need medical support. Now." A sudden crackle, then Dispatch reassures me that someone's on the way.

His skin is getting colder by the minute.

I force my hand against the jack in his head, then plug the meter in to read his vitals. The kid isn't going to make it to see the medic. The low signals flashing across the screen of my meter are redundant. I already know the score.

"I'm Haley." The girl is calm where others would be crying. She's stopped screaming. Where there were screams, I can hear only ragged, hollow gasps. I don't hear most of what she says next. Too busy finding the spot underneath his sternum. My hands start moving after that on their own.

They say that learning CPR is like riding a bicycle. I hope as I push down on his chest that they're right. His lips against mine taste sour. I can hear the meter beeping as I exhale into his mouth.

It beeps once, then twice, then it stops. And so do I.

"He's dead."

The door opens and more of the team comes barreling in. I step back, my hands raised, as the angels lean over him, clamping a mask over his mouth and reaching out for arms and wrists. One of them kicks the meter over to me. Her face is already sweating.

"Thanks, Shilo." I pick it up and put it in my pocket, then step backwards again, crowded out by the flock of pale coats. Haley - if it's really her name - stares at me as though she wants me to say something.

"Not my job," is all I manage before I walk out the door.

The headache. It's killing me. I'm seeing spots all through the next seven calls. I drag myself through the rest of the night trying to forget how long it took to wash the blood off my hands.

Not my job.

It wasn't. I make house calls. I'm the guy you call when you can't install a program, when your persona freezes, when your Net connection's slow. I'm not there to cradle a dying man while the lights on my meter blink on and off. But today, I was.

I think it's the look in her eyes that drives this spike through my skull. She should have been crying.

She wasn't.

The next night it's an old one.

I take the call even though they offered me a night off. I can't afford shell shock - the rent's too high in my part of town. Must be higher in the place I pass through - the buildings are so nice they don't even have windows. Why make them see the streets underneath?

This time, the caller opens the door himself. My hands stop shaking. Wiping my palms on my jeans, I ask what the problem is. A simple freeze. He can't access the internet from that jack in his head.

We sit side by side on a wooden bench in the hallway. I won't be asked to go out of sight of the front door. That's how these people are. His hands are shaking as he holds the meter for me. The plug slides in smoothly, the numbers flow like a pale green river across the screen. All is as it should be. Only a couple quick pecks on the meter and I solve it.

His fingers are quivering a little as I finish up. I can see that his lips are chapped when he thanks me. His hands are white paper with a tiny sliver of green between the palms.

What the hell. I take what I can get. The job doesn't pay enough.

The slamming of the door is all the farewell I need. Climbing back in the truck, I start to drive. If this was another neighborhood, I might stay, check the log book, call in even. But staying in a good neighborhood can be every bit as dangerous as wandering the bad.

It's an old truck but it gets me to 59th where I can see the dirty river as I pull over and check the book.

"Diego," My handset crackles. "Did you take the call on 32nd?"

"Yeah." I'm writing it in the book right now. No editorial comments. "Old man. Forsythe. Why?"

"He's calling back. Says he can't breathe."

"Call an angel. I'm just a runner, you know that."

"I know." The voice is clipped. I can't tell who it is over all the static. "Was he having trouble when you ran the diagnostic?"

"His hands got a bit pale. Course, he was already pretty white to start with." I cough, then shut the book. "Guy's got to be pushing sixty. On a good day."

"Just check in when you get back." Hands back on the wheel, I wait for the next instruction. "I've got another one for you. 4th and Jackson. This one just got a system and can't figure out how to install it."

"Nice." I mutter sarcastically. "I'll see ya when I see ya."

We call them angels because they're the last resort of us service techs. They're the ones we call in when someone's going to die. They call us runners because we run away when there's a real crisis. There's no love lost between us but like so many enemies in this town, we have to work together, like it or not. And with Shilo, that's a definite not.

"Nice day," she says. It's raining so hard I can't even see out the tiny window in the cafeteria. Before I can say anything to that, she's turned and gone, heels clattering towards a table in the corner where her eyes keep talking to me from across the room. They aren't nice words.

I take my tray and slide in by Mitch. Being a friend of his is like owning a neurotic dog. He's eager as he turns up his chin. I know he's heard something before he even says a word.

"Diego, you got a coder last night." He sounds like he's asking something even when it's a direct statement. Because of this, I shovel a piece of bread into my mouth, ignoring the question. Mitch leans forward. "Is that why Shilo was talking to you? Was she there when he died?"

I continue to eat. It's like swallowing chalk.

Mitch leans back and starts fiddling with his meter. I watch as he plugs himself in and stares at the signal for a few minutes, timing his breath. It's better than dieting, he once told me. He scratches the side of his head, then pokes me again. "Hey, this isn't working."

"Go to the bay and get a new one."

"Nah, I want to finish lunch. Just gimme yours for a second." I hand it over. At least when he's watching his biorhythms, his mouth stops moving. "God, you haven't up-graded this thing in ages."

"You don't like it, go talk to them." I hook a thumb towards the angels' table.

"I think I'll pass." He hands the meter back after shaking it a couple times, then stands up. "Get a drink after work, maybe?"

"Let me think about it," I say, although the answer's always yes.

"You think and I'll meet you there." Mitch shoves his hands in his pockets. "Later." He walks down the hallway, fading into the crack of light at its end. It isn't long before I follow.

He's not there.

Fine. So he's ditched me. I can take rejection. What I can't take is the look in Shilo's eyes as she walks towards the bar. She's so very pleased with herself that it makes me want to slap her.

"Diego." I nod. Angels don't deserve words. "I supp-ose you've heard about your calls." Another drink goes down my throat in response. "All dead, every one of them."

"Tell me this is a pathetic attempt to get me to speak to you." But the words alarm me. It can't be right. I've had over twelve calls the past two nights.

"The honest truth." Her teeth are sharpened pearls. "They hadn't told you? That's not the best sign, don't you think?" Blinded by the shock of it, I shove her backwards trying to get off the chair. I can't figure out why I believe her but I do.

"Come on, Diego. A reinstall? Even you should be able to figure that out." She's enjoying this. I can't breathe. "Unless you had something to do -" Shilo smells like tobacco as she leans against me. "I know you're not the only one who takes a little extra."

My shirt's never felt so tight before.

Then it happens. The same feeling as when I walked in on the dying boy. The world stops spinning and I can see her. Really see her. The cheap blue fabric of her shirt, the way her hair sits on her head, teased and permed so that it crackles like a stripped wire. It gives me the extra step I need to walk for the door.

"Find someone else to play with, Shilo." And I'm gone.

My fists are slamming so hard on the wheel that they hurt. She can't be telling me the truth. It feels like she's playing some game and that's what keeps me driving well beyond my street. When I finally stop, it's in front of Mitch's house.

"He isn't home yet." Josie says. She's in her bathrobe when she answers the door. I notice that she's still wearing her shoes as if she expects to be called out. "He's never late. I thought he was with you."

I hear the phone ring.

"I'll be right back." She shuts the door. I wait fifteen minutes. Maybe more. Then, when it doesn't open, I look down at my meter, then back at the apartment and something clicks inside. Or maybe it breaks.

A virus.

Computers get viruses. People don't. Not anymore. We still cough and sneeze but when all's said and done, that jack in our heads is what brings us closer to the outside world. And it's perfectly safe when we keep it in check. There's always some asshole ready to scan the nearest fourteen year old and there's always an idiot who tries to stick a key in their head socket to see what will happen but you and me? We're safe. We're totally secure.

Only…if the look on Josie's face is what I think it is…we're not.

I can't say anything to her. I can't even hold her when she cries. I did this. Me. That's why I have to run. She starts bawling when I turn away from her and sprint for the truck.

She doesn't understand. They haven't told her what I've done.

This is good. It means I have some time.

I trace the path in my head. I start with Mitch.

He used my meter. That was where it started. I used the thing on every call I made, just for checking rhythms. Then my mind flashes back. Back to the old man, to the cash he slipped me. To the call from dispatch right after. Back to the teenage girl right before it, chewing gum while I checked her. Snapping it in my ear.

Back to the floor and the darkness. That girl. Haley.

You wouldn't believe how fast you can make one of these trucks go. It's like quicksilver.

I don't knock- I kick it open.

She's alone, like I knew she would be. Only this time, the CDs are filling neat little boxes, each one marked with the names of countries. She doesn't look surprised to see me but disappointed. Like she expected me sooner.

"Tell me why you did it."

"I don't know what you're talking about." Haley closes another box. The girl doesn't look like a killer. Her legs are too thin, like twin reeds in the wind. They're shaking but her face doesn't look scared.

"But you stayed here." I'm walking towards her before I can even stop myself. I could hold her throat in one hand. "Did you think I wasn't going to find you?"

She pats one box, then tapes it shut.

"You're crazy," Haley says. "Go before…before I call someone."

"What's in the box?" I kick it. She jerks back from my foot as if I'm going for her next. Who knows? Maybe I am.

"Just a stupid game." Something catches in her throat as she says it. "Michael was testing it for someone. I'm just sending it on." I can see her breathing quicken as the words

84

come out of her throat. A game. Yeah, that's exactly what this is.

A haze clouds my sight as I look at her lying face. I can see a tiny drop of sweat fall on her nose. She knows what's on those discs and it's no toy.

My eyes close for a second and when I open them again, I've knocked her to the floor. Such a tiny woman. Like a butterfly. She's awake but just barely. She's soft where others are hard angles. I kneel next to her and watch her eyelashes move, so quickly I can tell she's afraid of what happens next. But you'd never know by the turn of her lips.

While she's lying there, I push a box towards her, crack it open, slitting the tape with one sharp nail. Each one of these has a different address written on it. I pull a CD out, look at the title. Conquest.

"Where's your machine?" I ask. She rolls her head to the side. The woman knows her own eyes will betray her. It's still in the same spot the man was holding it. I can smell his death on the thin black box- that scent doesn't wash away.

I look down at her, then smash the glass in on the meter. She flinches as I open the box then slide the CD inside.

It only takes a second to slide the plug into the jack underneath her blond hair.

"Should I run it?"

Her eyes widen. I can't tell if she thinks I'm crazy or if she knows about the virus from the look in them. Either option is her death sentence. I can see that she knows it.

I lean down, my finger hovering over the power button when I hear it. The door opening. For a moment, I expect her friend to walk in alive. That this has all been some joke. But life doesn't work that way.

It's Shilo.

"I didn't radio in," I start to say, then stop. She starts to fumble through her purse. She's obviously looking for a phone. Then it hits me. "It was you."

She stops.

"It was." A smile cracks her face. It's a thin hard line. "But you're the one standing over the body, Diego." I can see her fingers touch a few buttons on the phone. I reach her before she can speak, my hand clenching her wrist so hard it keeps her from opening her mouth for a moment.

"Turn it off." She does. I don't let go of her. She's a lot less fragile than Haley. She'd have to be, to dispose of the bodies. "Tell me why."

"Life doesn't work that way." Shilo sneers in my face. "You don't always get to know."

"So what? You're a serial killer?" The squeeze tightens. She wants to yelp - I can see it in her face. "Tell me."

"I'm trying to bring you down. All of you."

The words shock me so much I let her go. The woman just stands there for a moment, rubbing her wrist. Her eyes are glittering in the light of the door. I don't say anything, just watch her. She'll hang herself given enough rope.

She says a moment later, "It only takes one panic. And then no more runners, no more jacks in our heads, no more games to keep us dreaming." She raises a hand, points at the apartment. "Do you think they'd live like that if they had to actually *look* at it?"

I turn to see what she's pointing at. I can smell the air- it's like standing in a closet here. No pictures on the walls. A carpet that's matted. Stack of pizza boxes in the kitchen that's been there for weeks maybe. But it's bearable to the girl still lying on the floor because she can put a plug in that jack and leave. What I give her isn't technical support - it's freedom to dream.

And when I'm looking at Shilo again, she's holding a gun. I can already hear the sirens in the distance. It's like crying.

"Lie down." Her hand is shaking. It's easier to deal with a man when he's already dead. She hasn't killed before and stuck around for the act.

I jump.

I think I'm going to make it, that she won't have the nerve to fire for about thirty seconds before the gun goes off. Fire explodes in my stomach and I fall back, gasping. It's hard to breathe. When I look up at her, her face is frozen. I think she's going to lean down and help me but she doesn't. Instead, she leans down next to the girl and I hear another shot.

Shilo stands and uses the hem of her skirt to wipe the metal. It takes less than a minute. Then the gun falls to the floor between us.

By the time the medics rush up the stairs, she's crying loud jerking tears as I try to open my mouth. But I can't breathe. I want to tell them what she's done. But what I want most of all is to tell her. You can't take away a dream without giving a person something in return. It kills.

But looking at Shilo, I can see she already knows that. I close my eyes and try to gather the strength for a few words. If I only have enough time...

It takes six minutes for a brain to die.

It isn't enough.

HARD WONDER

Ian Donnell Arbuckle

I love waking up from nightmares. It's the best evidence I have for the truth of the adage: No pain, no gain. A tragedy, which hurts as much as the brain can handle when asleep, gets brushed away into something less than memory upon waking, and I feel as if I am starting a brand new life.

On the other hand, I hate waking up from pleasant dreams (which really deserve a catchy nickname, like "nightmares.") I have fallen in love in a dream or two in my time, and waking from those feels very similar to losing a relative.

Somewhere between those extremes lies Johnny Cousin, the protagonist of "Hard Wonder." He's one of those characters whose changes manifest not in any social, positional, or economic shift, but in the conviction he feels toward his stationary life. Somewhere in this is a bit of misguided rebellion from traditional character arcs.

I hope that doesn't seem boring to you, but, heck, I won't mind if you fall asleep during it, as long as you dream about something. Enjoy.

It was not a night to spare expense. The firm had defended against their twenty-fifth anti-trust suit earlier that afternoon and, to celebrate, the senior partners had brought out all the silver, and had sprung for the champagne. The party went through the natural life cycle of this sort of office party, starting with the tentative first introductions and flirtations, growing into the comfortable din of a dozen concurrent conversations, lapsing into silence as guests individually realized they had nothing more to say, and then dissipating as the elderly and the far too young slouched out under heavy felt coats and identical flat-brimmed hats. By three in the morning, the only ones left in the offices were the middle-aged, those not yet over the hill but right at the summit, and one young lawyer who wanted to ingratiate himself.

The brandy came out, as did the cigars, and soon, by the alcohol heat and Havana exhales, the men were pimpled with sweat over their laser-shaven cheeks. Their ties already were loosened, so they began unbuttoning their shirts and pumping the fabric over their chests like bellows, laughing and snorting and desperate not to fall asleep, for to sleep would be a waste of time.

When it got too hot to move, they started burning money. Everybody chipped in, emptying their pockets of chits until there was a pile the size of a pumpkin on the table between them. They took turns, as a family might take turns opening presents on Christmas morning, not out of a desire to see joy flash across their coworker's face, but to build up suspense, to revel in the fascination.

The young lawyer was last in the circle, and he had never burned with these men before. He stayed quiet, some small part of him fearing that the only reason he was still here was that they hadn't noticed him yet. He laughed at the right times -- for he was going places -- though never too loud, and he stared with the others as each man placed a chit against his temple and pressed, sending recorded electronic signatures through his brain, which scrambled to adapt to this new information and, quick as you can tell your lips to smile, copied wave for wave the emotion held inside the chit.

These were mostly wonders, joys, a few lusts, which were declining in value as the market realized that lust was not necessary to fabricate. It was almost the young lawyer's turn. He watched the features of the man to his right settle and soften until the skin was no good for holding back tears.

"Here Johnny," said the man on the young lawyer's left, passing him a chit. Johnny grinned, took it, and pressed it to his temple, his sweat sealing the connection. He didn't see the fist-shielded chuckles of the few men whose emotions had already wound down, and, though he heard the humor, it didn't sound out of place. He shot the chit, using up its charge, rendering it worthless.

Johnny Cousin wasn't stupid. He was going places. He was a capable lawyer; he spoke to juries as though they were his peers, and he did so on purpose. He had risen from assistantship to associate to trial lawyer in just a few years, and his first solo case was this coming Tuesday. He wasn't stupid. There are plenty of gullible people who aren't stupid.

The emotion hit him like a bullet -- that is to say so quickly that he couldn't identify nor examine it. He pitched forward and vomited. His spine crawled with the glares, the hunting focus of some invisible creature. He scrambled to his feet, slipping on the puke, and tried to run. He tripped over the armchair of a laughing attorney and fell into a crouch. His hands smelled like acid, like acid and alcohol.

"What'd you give him?" someone asked. "Oh shit, that's hilarious. You've got one of those? It's like a food stamp, brother."

"I found it in the gutter," someone else said.

Johnny sobbed into his hands and twisted up against a wall. There was a window. He slithered away from it, settling into a corner, his fingers laced over his eyes, too afraid to either open or close them.

"Should get this on camera. You got a camera?"

The dramatics were over, though. Johnny's terrified mind calmed like an ocean, a small derivative, the waves still present just less forceful. He pulled his hands away from his eyes and focused on the other men and their tucked-up playground leers.

Johnny wiped his chin on his sleeve; the shirt was ruined anyhow. "You bastards," he said as though he were in on the joke. "You royal bastards." And, far removed from his grudging laugh, he was thinking, And that's what he feels? My god. My god. What have I done?

"You receive a pension for your son's service, do you not?"

"For when he is released, ma'am, yes," said Johnny. Throughout the last couple of days he had been unable to stop thinking about how he had felt that night. Memory stands apart from pain, the same as a noun stands apart from the thing it represents. Still, the memory was potent and made his sinuses hurt. He hadn't been focused on his job, on the preparations for his trial on Tuesday. Some of his coworkers, the ones who had been there that night, had come up to him and nudged him in his ribs, joked about the look on his face, pulled their own faces into rude caricatures. Johnny's reserve of humor ran out in mere hours, and after that he just replied with, Yeah, that was great.

"And why do you want to terminate his employment prematurely?" Johnny was standing in front of the desk of a secretary to one of the senior partners; several steps removed from power, but he could feel it, the ability to effect a change, pulsing in the conditioned air.

The secretary was leaning forward on her desk, elbows on the blotter, her thin glasses centered on her eyes. She was young, or looked it; no more than a couple years older than Johnny. Her expression invited him to fill the silence; he chose to fill it with excuses.

"I didn't realize what I was doing. The tests said he gave strong reactions and would be ideal for the mint, but--"

"So you signed him over. Terror, you said?"

"Yes," said Johnny. The secretary nodded as if hearing from him a condemnation in that one syllable and agreeing with it, though not without sympathy. She pressed a finger into her right ear, the better to hear from the microspeaker embedded there.

"Excuse me for just one moment, mister Cousin." The secretary left through a door behind her desk. The door clicked shut. Johnny thought of shutting doors, of putting the past in its place and locking it there, of dark impenetrable wood behind which is hidden whatever you please, of the room in the corner in a corner of your house, out of sight so the mind can gradually flush its memories away.

The door opened; the secretary breezed back to her desk. She swiveled in her chair, settling it in the right position, then smiled.

"Did you know that they now manipulate their dreams, as well? So, in essence, they are working twenty-four hours a day. That must be . . . terrible." The secretary smiled again. "Or terrific, depending on who you are, I suppose."

"Yes."

Where Johnny would have rustled a sheet of paper or glanced at his watch, she fixed him on the two points of her eyes and waited for her next thought to form into words. "And your wife?" she said.

"We're no longer together," said Johnny.

"Good. That will make this less complicated."

"You can do something?"

"We can do something, mister Cousin. But it will require an effort on your part, as well. You like the work, don't you?"

"Yes," said Johnny, and it was partly true. He liked what the job allowed him to do; that is, he liked attending parties, and he liked being a part of the winning team, and he liked coming home way too late to a bottle of bourbon and a house, built large so as to enclose the maximum amount of silence, and with silence comfort.

The work itself was a tool, a commodity, something for him to sell in exchange for every docile fantasy he had.

"You have done a satisfactory job in the past few months. It hasn't escaped the notice of the senior partners."

"Thank you," said Johnny.

"Your first solo is on Tuesday, is it not?"

"That's correct," said Johnny.

"Good. The senior partners would like you to throw it."

"What? Why?"

"I hardly think I need tell you, mister Cousin, that in some instances there can come profit from loss." The secretary was smiling; her eyes said, I know you really are smart enough to know that, and Johnny almost believed her. An expression like that could have sold cars; it was so full of camaraderie, of earnest kinship born in shared experience.

"No," replied Johnny.

"Good. Do not turn it into a mistrial; that's the kind of cock-up nobody needs. Weaken your case, discredit your own witnesses, hem and haw to the jury. Make a few bad jokes." Her voice had taken on the mad Mosaic timbre of someone dispensing commandments from on high. Behind her words, Johnny could hear the low whine of the speaker in her ear. One of the senior partners telling her what to say; this woman existed only to keep supplicants at arm's length from the power. Johnny was not a praying man, but right then he wondered how frustrating it must have been to accompany each prayer with a sacrifice, an extra wing of potency, without which the prayer would flutter helplessly in the mezzanine, easy prey for circling doubts, far removed from the shrouded presence of the Old Testament god.

Johnny almost bowed as he left. On the way out, he passed a platinum reproduction of winged victory, she whose wings are the templates for all that flies. He reflected on the meeting -- his knees shaking as they had his first time addressing a judge -- and what it would cost him, which was, to his estimation, fairly large. A handful of terrors made a plastic chatter in his jacket pocket. He reflected, misshapen, in winged victory.

The guys in the office gave Johnny pats on the back and buck up pep talks. Everyone stopped by to congratulate him on a job well done, too bad the twelve went in for the other guy, but sometimes that can't be helped. Johnny was tired and gracious and said, Just gotta get back up on the horse, he couldn't guess how many times. The distractions came at fifteen minute intervals, sometimes the same guys more than once. No hard feelings, said the guy who had slipped him the terror that night, and it wasn't a question. No hard feelings, said Johnny, patting the chits in his pocket.

He was annoyed at the distractions, but he didn't know what he would have done without them. He couldn't concentrate on the work; his monitor kept deforming every time he blinked, waves of misguided electrons sheeting to the bottom. Somewhere in the office was a crying baby, and the susurrus of its client mother hushing it up, her sibilance matching the disturbed frequency of Johnny's screen.

His phone rang, throwing off the baby's howl, the mother's whisper. He answered it.

"Mister Cousin," said the secretary on the other end. "Have you been keeping up with the news?"

He hadn't been. Preparing for his case had been more important in the way that circumvents any method of prioritizing; but even without the thrown case, he wasn't much of a news hound. The things he needed to know filtered through other people to his ears, and at the end of the day he went home to a quiet house with no TV. He said as much, aware that outside of his head it sounded like rambling.

"Nine days ago, a vigilante group raided the Pac-Nor mint in Bellingham. The group's apparent aim was to liberate the staff. Your son was one of those liberated."

"Where is he, now?"

"Local police conducted an area search. You should read it for yourself. They turned up Contentment--" referring to the kid by the emotion she was tapped for "--huddled in an alleyway trying to wrap a sheet of rotten drywall around herself. The others didn't turn up in the county."

After a compliment on a job well done -- which felt to Johnny no more or less than the pats on the back -- the secretary hung up, saying she would leave him to it, whatever *it* was. His son was nine days gone from the mint. How far can a kid run in nine days? How far can a kid -- who has been stuck in his own mind for fifteen years and whose only experience with running has come from escaping the monsters that visited inside injected fever dreams -- go in nine days?

If it had been me, Johnny realized, I would have gone until my lungs caved in.

Rubbing his temples, he caught up on the news. As it turned out, some of the kids had gone home, authorities assuming the vigilantes had told them where to go. Anger burned a tree house down and was in custody. The mints didn't want the kids back, now; they were spoiled goods, once earthbound and now released into the great wide unknown. The air they had known would never taste the same again.

Johnny cut out early and sped home. He pulled onto his street with the sun in his eyes and saw the silhouette of his house undamaged and was relieved.

Grady pulled up out front in his near-silent car; Johnny wouldn't have noticed had he not been waiting for the man. It was a couple of weeks later, and Johnny still hadn't decided what to do about his son, who had taken to calling Trey, thanks to the circling strange abstraction of the brain which turns a word around until its syllables overlap and its meaning takes second seat to the sounds themselves.

He strolled down the front walk to greet Grady. Grady wasn't from around here; he wasn't an American. He spoke English haltingly and with a grammar all his own. He made you feel as though every gap in communication was your fault for not speaking clearly, while your brain protested that it was his fault for fouling up the language in his head. Still, he was the best private investigator in the area and he had worked with Johnny's firm on a number of occasions, so Johnny at least knew him by sight, as well as by his reputation.

He told himself he was collecting information, in order to make an informed decision, and couldn't help feeling as though he were betraying someone, or, more accurately, some *thing*, some wordless ideal. By not upping stakes and running to Bellingham? he asked himself. Unreasonable, misguided, emotional. Came the response: how better to find your son, who has lived his whole life unreasonably, without guidance, submerged in an emotion much more powerful -- therefore more valuable -- than the paternal instinct.

"Nice car," said Johnny as he extended his hand to Grady. Grady took it, then released it as though he had decided not to shake after all. He turned and examined his car from hood to trunk, then returned his attention to Johnny.

"Yes," he said. "I enjoy a good car."

"What is it? A Freya roadster, right? Love the color."

"Good running," said Grady. "Take me inside." He was holding a black leather briefcase in one hand. He used it to gesture at Johnny's house.

"Right. Please, come in," said Johnny.

Grady went immediately to the dining room table and sat, opening his briefcase and laying out a series of contracts and forms for Johnny to sign. Johnny, meanwhile, got himself a drink.

"Want a drink?" he asked.

Grady waved his negative. "For the driving," he said. "Sign your life," he said, tapping his finger on the nearest sheet of paper, then pulling a pen from his breast pocket and repeating the gesture.

"Excuse me?" Johnny took a sip of his drink and sat down opposite Grady.

"Sign your life," said the PI. "For payment."

Johnny couldn't quite place Grady's accent. There were the rolled Rs, the swallowed vowels of Russia; but he also tended to emphasize the second syllable, as Germans or Scotsmen do. The man's looks didn't clear anything up. His hair was gray, but looked as though it could have been artificially so. His eyebrows were triangular, pointing upwards, shadowing his eyes. His face was smooth and square and carried the sort of contemplative neutral expression that once upon a time may have caused swoons in the girls of his native land, wherever that was.

"Sign my life?" said Johnny. Grady stared at him, licked his lips, blinked, returned to staring. Johnny bent and started reading the contracts. When he was halfway through, Grady spoke.

"I am going from America," he said. "Tell the word around. After your money. I am going." Johnny kept reading. "Stupid America," Grady went on. "Sensitive to light, to shadow, to food. Babies that cry. And worthless money."

"Worthless," said Johnny, glancing meaningfully around his sleek unsullied rooms.

"Gold is worthless," said Grady. "No bullets to be made, no walls will stand. Too soft. So is your new money. Worthless."

"Is that why you ask for so much of it?" Johnny had finished reading the contracts. Grady grinned, boxy teeth shoving his lips apart. He replied something about moving that Johnny didn't understand and let disappear without response. He began inking his initials and names over the sheets of the contract.

When he was finished, Grady collected his copies and snapped them into the briefcase. Johnny wrote up a bank authorization, asking, "What do you want it in?"

"Wonder," said Grady. Johnny made it so and handed over the note.

"Remember," he said. "I don't want him to know that his dad is looking for him. I mean, I don't know what he'd do. I don't want him to run. Just tell me where-- just tell me if he's all right and where he is."

Grady nodded. "It's in the contract." He let himself out.

Johnny sat hunched forward on his couch, elbows on his knees. He listened to Grady's car purr off. After a while, he got up and, shoving the loose contract aside, opened his own briefcase and caught up on a little work, scribbling notes with one hand while the other made plastic chirps with the terror in his pocket.

Three weeks later, Grady was sitting on Johnny's couch, sipping a water. Johnny was sitting across from him on the corner of the coffee table, flipping through the pages of notes and photographs that Grady had brought with him.

"Oliver Kyle Cousin," said Johnny.

"He names himself O.K.," said Grady.

"He kept the surname."

Johnny looked at the face of his son and recognized nothing in its features. It was wholly unique -- a stranger's face, smiling, holding a milkshake in one hand. A girl was sitting next to him with her chin in her netted finger, dimly reflecting O.K.'s smile.

"Who is the girl?" asked Johnny.

Grady had a mouthful of water. He spit it back into the glass. After a length of silence, Johnny looked up from the picture to see what was taking so long. Grady was rubbing two wonders together between his thumb and middle finger. He nodded significantly at the chits. Johnny got the hint. Grady slipped the chits back into his pocket.

"Her house," he said. "He eats next to her and sleeps in her window."

"In her window?"

Grady took another drink of water. He made a face of disgust and spit this mouthful out, too.

"I am done," he said. "Yes. Tell the word around. No more days of your independence. No more of your wives, daughters, husbands, and sons. I hate. You are the last I hate. I am tired of this hate. I need new hate, far from here." He stood up, placing his glass on the table next to Johnny. Johnny didn't move. "Look at you," said Grady. "You are sitting. This is why I will leave America. Your son is in your hand and you sit down."

Johnny picked up the water glass and set it on a coaster. Then he looked up. "You don't understand. A decision can't be rushed; time has to pass."

"No. An idiot would say so. Decisions, such as decisions in a court, yes, are made long before time. Guilty, yes?"

"What are you saying?"

Grady smiled thinly, in that instant so like a grandfather, dying, prepared to leave behind a legacy of righteous fury if nothing else would stick.

"I say you should have no secrets from your son."

Then Grady left, taking his echoes with him. Johnny moved to the couch. He thought, for quite some time, in two minds: one was a scale weighing the choices that were in front of him; the other sat in judgment on the first, growing ever more blood-fired and angry that he could even consider there to be a choice in the matter at all.

Wonder -- the kid's name was Delicate Jones -- and her folks lived a bit north of Ashland, Oregon. According to Grady's report, she and O.K. had jumped freight trains down from Bellingham. A conductor had spotted them in Portland, recognized them from their photos on the news, but hadn't told the authorities; turned out he was a disgruntled citizen and had taken some pride at telling Grady of his naughty deed. The kids had thanked him. He said that the girl looked tired and was huddled into the guy. She may have been sick. The guy seemed all right. Both of them were bald.

Johnny spent the plane ride reading the report and, once the words began the give him a concentration headache, gazing at the pictures. There was one of O.K. and Delicate seen from a distance; they were sitting on the green hill of some park. It was taken on a sunny day, but they were pressed together, sealing all space between them like two hands clenched together, as though a blizzard were falling around them.

On the ground, Johnny checked into a hotel in Ashland. He ate a quick dinner in the hum of a Shakespeare-themed restaurant. He had Steak-upon-Onions. He left the waitress, who had had bad comedic timing, a joy, though he thought she'd probably burn it with her friends later that night. It was dark by the time he returned to his hotel and lay on the room's thin bed.

The street ran close to his first-floor window. The sound of passing cars didn't so much bother him as the vibrations that they transmitted from street to earth to wall to bed. He found himself unable to sleep. More than once he was close, but each time came a youth with a perversely loud bottom end, or a diesel hauler, and startled him so that he felt his eyes yanked back to him from dreamland as if they were attached to his sockets by rubber bands.

He turned on the TV to distract himself. He found a movie that, after a few lines, he recognized as being one that his co-workers frequently quoted to each other around the office. It was awful. There was a laugh track.

Johnny got out of bed. When he wasn't lying down, he didn't feel the vibrations so strongly. They passed through his feet, up his tibia and then, though he didn't realize it, were obliterated by the quaking in his knees.

In the end, he just went ahead and did it. He waited around a frozen yogurt shop Grady had observed the kids frequenting and got a coffee. He was there when the shop opened at ten in the morning; he kept ordering coffees until O.K. and Delicate slouched in at two. Johnny tried not to look at O.K. as his son waited in a short line to order for the both of them. Delicate sat down at a table in the corner and leaned her head against the wall. She had eyes as round and dead as two pennies. Her hair was coming in, a light blonde fuzz. She was staring right at Johnny. After a few moments, he tried giving her a wink, but it wasn't something he had practiced and it felt slow and weak.

O.K. slid into the seat across from her, back to his father. He talked quickly, barreling over the cracks in his pubescent voice. He had stories to tell -- dreams to be remembered in the sugared cool air, to be exposed for the absurdities they were. He had a phrase that Johnny had never heard before: Cut the rope, man. He said it over and over. The whole shop heard them; Johnny caught the cashier grinning once. He went up to get another coffee.

"That kid come in a lot?" he asked.

"O.K.? Yeah. He's new around here. Kid has the strangest dreams. My brother owns a bookshop on seventh; I keep trying to get O.K. to show up for the open mic nights. He'd be a treat."

When Johnny sat down, he chose a table closer to the kids. Now he could hear Delicate, too, with her soft interjections. Her laugh came through her nose in soft chuffs like a dog sighing. O.K. had a laugh that filled the room with descending cadences. Sometimes he slapped the table, setting their spoons to vibrating.

"Let's go to the park," O.K. suggested when their dishes were empty. Delicate nodded. She moved as though through gauze, and her slow eyes seemed clouded by the same. O.K. took her hand and escorted her out the door. Johnny followed.

The kids walked, O.K.'s right hand entwined with Delicate's left. With his free hand, O.K. gestured and pointed, as though conducting a symphony of his own words. The park was nearby, not much more than a small hill on a triangular lot bordered by traffic. The kids sidestepped a pair of frolicking dogs and a sunbather on her stomach with her top undone. Johnny leaned against a tree just off the sidewalk.

O.K.'s hand came unbound from Delicate's and signaled a crescendo of his laughter. Delicate shook her head, mock dismayed at whatever joke O.K. had just told. Her eyes settled on Johnny. He tried to turn away, but his own traitor eyes kept flicking back to the top of the hill to see if it was safe, if she had let her gaze drift. She hadn't.

So Johnny took a walk. Three blocks to the south, six blocks north, three blocks south again. He ended up at the same tree. The kids were still there, but lying on their backs, looking up at the few wispy clouds that were too faint and too high to be images of anything. Nevertheless, O.K. was pointing, tracing designs.

Johnny went halfway up the hill, past the sunbather, who looked up at him and smiled, and sat within earshot of the kids. They were silent. In that moment, Johnny was nearly content. The silence of the sun light and the silence of the children and the silence of the woman on her stomach were heavy like a drowsy lover's body. Even the noise of traffic almost faded into background, but then the profane honking of a horn made his heart beat arrhythmic and he coughed to set the pumping right again.

A swish of fabric came from behind. He turned in time to catch Delicate, in her flowered summer skirt, approaching. He leaned back onto his elbows, feigning comfort. She sat down beside him, cross-legged.

"I know what you want," she said. She didn't look up. "You want him." The conviction in her voice was like an order. Johnny took a breath to tell her what a crazy kid she was, but she turned her face away as though expecting his protest and refusing to accept it. She stared at O.K. She spoke haltingly, and she slurred as though her tongue were too slow for the thoughts that propelled it. She said, "Please. I love him," and, "I need him." She turned back to Johnny, who had lost all thoughts now of anything but silence, and squeezed her eyes shut, working the muscles to force saline onto her eyelashes, staining them dark brown. She said, "I wake up," and, "In the morning and all I have to do is roll over," and, "I can see him through my window, on the grass," and "You don't know me," and, "I used to be an angel. Yeah, I used to be an angel," and, "Now I'm not. I need to roll over and see him. I feel so lost in the morning. It's like heaven pulls back in the night," and, "This boring world -- I need him. Please. I need him. You adults can change things. You can change people. I think I understand. Please don't change him," and, "Please please don't look at him again."

She smelled of hospital air, thick with uncertainty, sickness, and skin. For her sake, Johnny resisted an urge to glance over his shoulder.

"I just wanted to apologize. Will you tell him--"

"No, please, no I won't," said Delicate. Then she stood up and her dress played a hush over the grass and Johnny heard her say, Hey wake up sleepy head.

That was that, then. Johnny stood up. He dug in his trouser pocket for a pair of wonders. He tossed them lightly on the grass where they'd find them if they returned the way they came.

Again, he didn't sleep that night. He paced, thinking of writing a letter to O.K., imagining the thousands of expressions that could cross his son's face upon reading it, and about how only one would. He went for a walk and wound up at the late night mall. Shaved heads were in this year. He saw versions of O.K. in every shop, all hunch-shouldered and loud and leaning in towards a girl's affections.

At the arcade and dumped his pocketfuls of terror on a little boy and his friend, saying, He doesn't need this anymore. The kids' faces lit up for a moment before they realized how worthless all that plastic was to them. Johnny watched them lug it to the counter and trade it into a couple tokens for the games; then he watched them spend the tokens on nightmarish pops of color and gunfire.

In the morning, he took a cab to the airport and bought a ticket home. While he waited for his plane to board, he leaned against the observation windows, watching the jets coast back and forth across the tarmac, swept-back wings summoning the constant illusion of movement, of speed, of victory.

FADE AWAY AND RADIATE

Justin Stanchfield

It's funny how some music sticks with you through the years. The title of this story comes from an old Blondie song. It was never released as a single, received no air time, and certainly wasn't a hit, but it has been lodged in my memory since I was in high school. My girlfriend - later my wife - gave me the album, Parallel Lines, and I listened to it until the tape became unplayable. But of all the songs on it, 'Fade Away and Radiate' was the one that I recall most clearly. Something about the way Debbie Harry's voice interacts with the droning, almost hypnotic synthesizer riff, or the slow, heartbeat pound of the kick-drum, that even today invokes a kind of sweet despair that carries me back to that other time. That other place.

Dull pain. Grinding, throbbing ache. Jack Spehar groaned softly, his head pounding as if wet leather had been wrapped around his skull and left to dry in the August sun. His eyelids seemed glued together, and when he tried to open them, the light that spilled through the slit pierced with the rapid-fire thrust of a nail-gun.

"Take it easy," a man's voice, vaguely familiar, said nearby. "Give yourself a chance to acclimate."

"Acclimate to what?" Jack replied, but the words came out a jumble, barely recognizable as speech. Ignoring the offered advice, he rose to his hands and knees. Immediately, a surge of vertigo crashed through him. Panicked, he toppled forward.

"Whoa!" The man who had warned him not to move now grabbed him by the collar and pulled him to the side, then gently lowered him back to the sun-baked earth. "Just lay still, okay? Give yourself some time."

"Where am I?"

"Not where. When. I'll explain later."

Still half-blind, Jack glanced up. He knew the face above him, but his mind refused to accept it in context. Certain he was losing his mind, he shielded his eyes from the glare and studied the face more carefully. Thin, with sandy-hair badly in need of cutting. A patchy, unkempt beard hid a weak chin, but his hazel eyes remained as piercing and clear as the last time Jack had seen him two years earlier.

"Cohen?"

The man nodded, a grim smile on his lips.

"But," Jack fought down a wave of nausea. "You can't be here. You're at Ganymede."

Again, the man nodded. "I'll explain later."

"No. Now." Despite the kiln-hot air, Jack shivered, chilled to the bone. Slowly, memory returned. He recalled being at the lab, drowsy from the tranquilizers, strapped tight to the narrow table as it slid into the tunneling chamber. More remembered sensations arrived. Vibration as the scanner engaged, the skin-prickling sensation of bees swarming across his face. Hot light, an incandescent blue so bright it burned his retinas through his closed eyelids. More shivering wracked him, and he felt his lips begin to tremble. A new thought struck him, terrifying in its implications. Chills and nausea were some of the first symptoms of radiation poisoning. Struggling against his own lack of equilibrium, he managed to sit up. "The lab? Was there an accident?"

"No. Not that I'm aware of," Michael Cohen said.

"I... I was supposed to go to Ganymede."

"I'm sure you did."

"I've got to get back" Jack tried to stand, but his muscles refused to support him, and Cohen once more lowered him to the ground. Small rocks and bits of prickly, dried grass gouged his cheek, but he was too miserable to care. "For God's sake, help me get back."

"Jack, damn it," another voice said, a woman's voice, sharp with the nasal twang of a New Englander. He knew it instantly. "Shut up and listen to Michael."

Sicker than he had ever felt in his thirty-seven years, Jack Spehar rolled over far enough to see the woman. Like Cohen, she was thin, her yellow blouse ratty and faded. Her gray-white hair was tied neatly into a tight ponytail, her face heavily lined. The same horrible confusion struck at him again. "Helen? You can't be here."

The woman and Cohen exchanged a quick, almost furtive glance. She knelt down beside him, her shadow mercifully blocking the sun. Helen Grieves sighed. "It's complicated. I'll explain everything when you're feeling better. Right now, rest. Get your strength back. Trust me, you're going to need it."

Clouds passed overhead, dull curtains nearly the same milky shade of blue as the listless sky. Jack stared up from the ground, half expecting to see vultures wheel overhead. Slowly, the sickness and the headache were receding, as were the chills, baked out of him by the relentless sun. This, the fact that the sun hung near zenith instead of low against the jagged southern horizon, confused him more than anything. It had been early February when he entered the chamber, the world outside the reinforced concrete walls that surrounded the apparatus frozen beneath a crust of ice-hard snow. If he had actually arrived at Ganymede, he wouldn't have seen any sun at all, but rather the interior of another chamber, bland and gray, housed deep within the satellite's icy crust. Instead, he lay on open ground, soaking up the heat of a summer day, the dusty air and flavored by the sulphurous stench of diesel smoke. Somewhere in the distance, a truck rumbled past.

"Where am I?" Jack's voice cracked. "Please. I need to know."

"All right." Helen Grieves helped him sit up. It took more effort than he had expected. Another wave of vertigo swept through him and he thrust his hand to the ground beside him for support, but recoiled as his palm pressed against the rocky soil. Something about it felt wrong, as if the dry, cracked earth was effervescing under him. He snatched his hand off the ground and wiped it on the leg of his soft blue sweat pants.

"Jack?" She leaned closer. "Do you recognize this place?"

"I think so." He let his gaze wander from left to right. Southward, a range of mountains, their barren granite summits hazy in the distance, rose above a vanguard of timbered foothills. To his left, eastward, stood another ridge, bisected by the diagonal slash of a highway curving upward along its flank. To the right, another steep hill thrust up, a few houses scattered along its base. Everywhere around him lay sagebrush, the valley floor choked with the tangled, knee-high scrub. He didn't need to turn around to know an enormous open-pit mine filled the northern horizon, the mountain's flesh stripped away to reveal a banded skeleton of pink and blue and mottled gray bedrock, the city that fed the mine with workers and resources perched perilously close to the mile-wide crater.

"Butte, Montana, right?" he said.

"Yes." A trace of hesitation hung in her tone, and again she exchanged a worried glance with Cohen. Jack noticed how much older she looked, new wrinkles around her eyes and the corners of her lips that hadn't been there last year when she, like Cohen and later himself, slid into the tunneling chamber. She swallowed, as if it took real effort, then continued.

"Yes. You're still in Butte. Do you notice anything else?"

Jack nodded. He had lived here nearly half a decade, long enough to recognize the area. But, while the distant skyline seemed unchanged, the foreground was as alien to him as the desiccated plains of Mars. Instead of the clustered grouping of concrete and steel laboratories that should have littered the flat, a handful of unfamiliar warehouses, several still under construction, stood nearby. A stretch of gravel road curved off his left shoulder, and as he watched, a tractor-trailer loaded with fresh cut logs drove into view, dust billowing behind it. It rattled with an ominous growl as the driver slowed for the approaching intersection. Jack flinched. It had been ages since he had heard a jake-brake.

"What year is it?" he asked quietly, barely able to whisper.

"1979," Cohen said. "August."

"1979." Jack repeated the simple string of numbers, as if incanting them might reconfigure the impossibility of what clearly stood before him. If Cohen was being truthful - and for the moment Jack had to assume he was - his own birth lay fifteen years in the future. The complex he had worked at for the last five years, the laboratories and generators and the massive focusing array were undreamt in even the wildest theoretical musings of this time. The idea that he had gone not to distant, frigid Ganymede, but instead been displaced fifty years into the past curdled in his stomach. Feeling ill, he turned back toward Helen. "How?"

"We always knew it was a possibility." She rose stiffly to her feet, then bent down and took his arm, hauling him upright. Jack swayed, but managed to stand on his own. She sighed. "The equations don't prohibit the movement of particles through time. But, we assumed that any temporal discharge would be random, a transient effect that dissipated instantaneously. Instead, it seems that a significant number of coupled particles are displaced in a time-wise direction during transmission."

"Okay," Jack said, struggling to understand. "So, instead of going to Ganymede, I wound up here." He had been an electrical engineer at the facility, his expertise the fine-tuning of the dish array that pushed the packets of information that would be reassembled into the complexity of a human being at the terminal end of the tunnel. Helen Grieves, like Cohen, was a theorist, one of the scientists who headed the project, and while he understood the basics of the concepts, the actual equations that lay behind the process were as unfathomable to him as the schematics he used would have been to her.

"Jack," Helen said softly. "You did go to Ganymede, just as Michael and the others did." She smiled ruefully. "I assume I made it there as well?"

He nodded, remembering the truncated, slow-motion conversations he had with her over the last eighteen months since she had tunneled to their sister facility on the Jovian moon. Creases furrowed above the bridge of his nose as the paradox struck him. "You're right. I've talked to you a hundred times. You're on Ganymede. How can you be here?"

"The same way you are." Her smile did little to drive the worry from her eyes. "You did go to Ganymede. The real you. The you here, at this point in time, is a displacement artifact."

"We're echoes, Jack," Cohen said.

"Echoes?"

"Yes." Helen put her hand on his shoulder. "Come on, let's get back to the others."

"Others?" Jack stiffened. "What others?"

"All of them," Helen said impatiently. "Everyone who has tunneled. We've all left an echo. Come on, it's going to be evening soon. Let's go."

Too confused to object, Jack fell in step behind Helen, Cohen remaining discreetly behind him, no doubt ready to catch him should he fall. Together, they marched toward one of the steel-sided warehouses. Long shadows cut across the ground as they neared the yellow and white building and climbed a set of stairs onto the truck dock that jutted from the side of the structure. A large, square door stood open, and they stepped inside. Jack blinked, his eyes adjusting to the dimmer light.

"This is part of our facility, isn't it?" he asked.

"Yes," Helen said. Their footsteps clicked and echoed around the empty space. "This is Building Seven. It was part of the original MHD project. We took it over when we inherited their labs." Jack nodded absently. MHD had been their precursor, a Department of Energy project studying the possibility of extracting electricity from coal via magneto hydro-dynamics. Later abandoned, the facilities had seemed the perfect location for the tunneling project, though it was hard to reconcile this empty shell with the building he recalled. The last time he had seen it, three days earlier, it was filled practically floor to ceiling with quantum computer banks and cooling units.

She led him deeper into the shadowed bay, then around a corner at the back of the structure. A wooden wall had been erected inside, the naked 2x4's so fresh they still oozed pitch, leaving a fresh, turpentine aroma in the air. No door hung in the framed entrance, the interior of the annex bare except for a pair of sawhorses stacked one atop the other. Sunlight angled through the single window, gilding the floor with the late-afternoon glow. Again, Jack blinked, startled to see a crowd of people waiting.

Nine men and women stood in a rough semi-circle, dressed in comfortable but tattered clothes, most likely the same clothes they had been wearing when they tunneled. All of them had the same hungry, tortured look to their gaunt faces.

"Hello, Jack." A stocky, bearded man with a fringe of collar-length gray hair circling his bald head, stepped forward. His voice was deep, authoritative, heavily accented by his native Russian. Victor Kalikov, like Helen Grieves, was one of the theoreticians who had moved into administration. Two years earlier he had been promoted to Coordinator and subsequently transported to Ganymede to oversee the work there. At the time, Jack had been glad to see him go. He was an autocrat, seldom willing to compromise, a sharp-tongued martinet with a caustic, biting wit.

He was also, Jack recalled, the first person after the test-pilot, to have tunneled. A sad smile lifted the corner of Kalikov's broad mouth. "I wish we were meeting under better circumstances."

"Hi," Jack finally managed to stammer. Before he could say more, the sound of footsteps outside the half-finished office made him spin around. A burly man in a stained T-shirt, a leather tool-belt slung around his hips, poked his head through the open door. He looked around, then, without comment, left. Jack stared in shock. "Who the hell was that?"

Kalikov shrugged. "One of the construction people. They always check the buildings before quitting time."

"He acted like he didn't see us."

"He didn't," Helen said without inflection. "From his reference, we aren't here."

"But," Jack's head began to swim. "How is that possible?"

"Like we told you," she said, softer now. "We're echoes."

"We are," Kalikov added, "only moderately reactive."

"Moderately reactive? What the hell does that mean?"

"It means," Helen explained, stepping closer, "that we won't sink through the floor, and we can't walk through solid walls. If we really work at it, we can sometimes move small objects. But that, apparently, is it. We are not fully connected to this space-time. We *feel* like we have solid, physical bodies, but from the viewpoint of 1979, we are little more than diffraction patterns.

The room seemed to tilt, and Jack spread his legs wider to keep from falling. Slowly he began to understand exactly what was happening, that he was trapped in a past he could not participate in. He licked his lips, his mouth horribly dry.

"Do you have any water?" he asked. An embarrassed silence fell around the little room.

"I'm sorry," Kalikov said, "but we don't. Even if we could find a way to bring it here, we couldn't raise the glass to drink. But, it is of little concern."

"You can't live without water," Jack protested.

"We can," Helen said softly. "The thirst you're feeling, or hunger or cold? They're an effect, something akin to what an amputee feels when they complain about pain in a missing limb. I suppose, eventually, our bodies might succumb to starvation, but it hasn't happened yet, and some of us have been here a long time."

The words, 'some of us' struck Jack odd, the phrase somehow insidious. Quickly, he did another head-count, silently naming each person in the room. A cold fear squeezed the wind from his lungs as he realized at least one person who should have been here, wasn't. "Where's Cutler? You said everyone who transmitted to Ganymede was here. He was the first person to go. He should be here, too, right? Where is he?"

Helen exchanged an uneasy look with Kalikov, then said, "Jack, try to understand…"

"Try to understand," Kalikov cut her off. "We are not actually here. We are electro-magnetic artifacts, and we are not permanent. Eventually we…" He faltered, searching for words. "We fade away. If it is any consolation, the process does not appear to be painful."

If the Russian said more, Jack didn't hear it, his ears filled with a high, undulating ring. Dizzy, he stumbled backwards and would have fallen had he not struck the wall. Again, the slick, effervescent sensation he had noticed earlier rippled through his flesh. He tried to push away, but his legs had gone numb and he began to sink to the floor. Cohen grabbed him and brought him upright once more.

"We've got to get out of here." Jack broke away from his grip. "We can't just sit here and wait to 'fade away' for God's sake!"

"Unfortunately," Kalikov said without the slightest bit of emotion. "Whether we like it or not, that is precisely what is going to happen."

They slept on the floor without blankets, huddled together for warmth. Despite whatever Helen Grieves might have insisted, Jack thought as he drew his arms tighter to his body, this cold felt all too real. He couldn't begin to imagine what it must be like to face the coming winter without coats, gloves or decent footwear. The previous winter, those stranded here had moved, she explained, to the lobby of a nearby motel to escape the worst of the weather. When he had pressed further about why they returned to this place, she had reluctantly explained.

"We don't have any way to know who, or when, the next person will arrive. But, we need to be here when they do."

"You didn't know I was coming?"

"How could we?" Helen shrugged. "We don't have a schedule. Do you?"

He had thought about it. "I know Carrara is supposed to go next, but it probably won't be until next month. His wife is expecting."

"And that," Helen had said, smiling, "is precisely the reason we keep vigil out there in that blasted lot. We don't know when someone will appear, only that at some point, they will."

Darkness had fallen by then, the nine - no, ten, Jack had to remember to include himself - had simply sat down to wait out the night. Little conversation was heard, as if they had long ago exhausted every topic and no longer bothered with the pretense. He replayed what he had been told, searching for any glimmer of hope. So far, he had found none.

"This is insane," he muttered, his voice lost among the scuffle and snores of the people nestled in the corner of the unfinished office. "It can't be happening."

"Jack? Is that you?" Helen said sleepily.

"Yes."

"Can't sleep?"

"No." He laughed sourly. "If I had known what was coming, I would have brought a pillow."

She laughed with him, a tired, defeated laugh, the laughter of someone who had watched their own hopes flicker and die like a candle on a windy night. He propped himself on his left elbow. Even in the dim light that spilled through the window, he was able to pick her out.

"Helen, listen." He hesitated, choosing his words carefully. "We have to find a way to contact our own time so they can stop tunneling."

"There isn't any way."

"But..."

"Don't you think we've been over this? Trust me, there's nothing we can do."

"I'm sorry, but I don't buy it. Christ almighty," Jack said, exasperated with her attitude. "You're some of the smartest people on the whole damned planet! There has to be some way to get word of what's happening back to our time."

"Let it rest, okay? Please?" Helen sighed loudly, but Jack noticed a hint of anger in her tone, as if the subject had become taboo. He let it drop, but decided to press her again in the morning when he could get her away from the others. Exhausted and cold, he drifted back to sleep and dreamt of home.

A narrow stream ran not far from the site, the bottom choked with thick, beige sludge, waste materiel washed downstream by decades of mining. Jack stared at the ripples, diamond bright in the morning sun, his parched throat screaming for a long, cool drink.

"Don't," Helen said as if she had read his mind. Startled, he spun around to face her. She smiled grimly and pointed at the creek. "The water is toxic. There's enough heavy metal in there to sink a battleship. God knows what it would do to you if you drank it."

"What difference would it make? The way you described it last night, we're just waiting to wink out anyhow."

To his surprise, she gave no argument, but instead joined him on the bank of the muddy stream. Behind them, separated by a sagging barb-wire fence, a car barreled down the gravel road. Jack watched it until it was nothing but a roiling dust cloud merging into the outskirts of town. He shut his eyes and tried to convince himself that all of this, the sights and scents, were nearly half a century old, a rerun of an old program played on a cosmic level.

For a while, he and Helen Grieves sat side by side, neither speaking. They had never been close, at least not in a

116

social sense, before she had left for Ganymede. The difference between their status on the project created an uncomfortable gulf between the scientists and the mere technicians, like himself. Somehow, Jack suspected, that equation had changed, the balance shifted. Now, they were comrades in arms, castaways adrift on a barren sea. They might never become friends, but he sensed a kindred spirit. He cleared his throat and looked at her.

"I've been thinking about what you said last night, about not being able to contact our own time?"

"Let it rest."

"I can't." He paused. "What was it you couldn't say around the others? You said it yourself that we can manipulate matter, at least in a marginal sense. And if that's true, there's a chance of getting a message through, right?"

She didn't reply immediately, but instead simply sat, staring down at the gurgling water. Absently, he watched her fingers dig into the sandy ground, then as quickly draw away. She turned and looked at him, the green of her eyes deepened by the water reflected in them.

"You have to understand," she began, her voice little more than a whisper, "We really have been over this a thousand times. Are there theoretical ways we might contact our own time? Certainly. If we could make ourselves noticed, and if we could find a place to leave a warning that we can know with certainty will be found X number of years from now. But, that doesn't necessarily mean we should."

Jack frowned. "What are you getting at? That we shouldn't warn them? For God's sake, this is inhuman, and it's only going to get worse. What happens when tunneling becomes commonplace? There will be thousands of us stranded like this, just waiting around to die. If there is any way we can put an end to it..."

"Listen." She cut him off. "You have to look at things from a bigger viewpoint. Yes, what happened to us - what is happening - is terrible. But, think of the benefits that tunneling can bring. The ability to transmit not only matter, but living, breathing human beings over the sort of distances that we're dealing with is among the greatest scientific breakthroughs in history. We can't just throw that away because of what is little more than a by-product."

"Are you listening to yourself?" Jack gaped at her. She looked away, unable to meet his gaze, an embarrassed flush creeping into her drawn cheeks. He had the sudden impression that Helen Grieves was voicing not her personal feelings, but simply repeating the party line. "So, there is a way to end this, but you've arbitrarily decided not to because it would shut things down. Nice."

"We... we took a vote."

"A vote?" He turned and stared toward the empty lot where he had materialized yesterday. The others stood there now, milling about listlessly. Only one figure seemed to have any purpose, directing the people around him with curt nods or gestures. Even as he watched, Victor Kalikov turned and faced where he and Helen sat, arms folded across his thick chest in an almost defiant posture. Jack snorted derisively. "Let me guess whose side won the election."

"Victor can be very persuasive when he wants," Helen agreed.

"You mean he bullied you into letting this charade go on." Jack drew a long, deep breath. He needed to think rationally, not let his emotions run away. "Fine, you all decided not to take any action that would jeopardize the project. Just tell me this much..."

Helen kept her face pointed at the muddy creek in front of her, but her eyes moved until she now watched him, waiting for him to continue. Jack smiled for her benefit, then asked, "If you did decide to act, what would be the best way to send a message to the future?"

She sighed, her eyes fixed once more on the rippling stream. Instead of answering his question directly, Helen asked, "Did I ever tell you where I grew up?"

Confused, Jack shook his head. She continued.

"I was born in Connecticut, but when I was twelve, my father took a professorship at the local college. I spent the next six years, until I graduated from high school, here, in Butte."

Jack sat up straighter as her words sank in. "You're here now? Your younger self, I mean?"

She nodded, the gesture so slight it was nearly invisible.

"Okay." Jack brightened. "If I can contact you in this time frame, that would change what's going to happen in ours?"

A faint smile crept across her worn features. "Let's just say it's theoretically possible." She sighed, then climbed stiffly to her feet and walked back toward Kalikov and the others. Jack watched her go, his mind spinning with what she had told him.

The day passed in a tangled blur. Without any concrete plan, Jack had slipped away from the others and hurried toward town, walking along the trash littered barrow pit. He had expected Kalikov to send someone after him, and when that didn't happen, he slowed his pace. By the time the gravel road had merged with blacktop, sweat ran down his back. A graveyard lay to his right, the weathered headstones shaded by gnarled cottonwood trees and neatly tended rows of lilac. The skin on the back of his neck prickled, unable to shoo away the idea that real ghosts might be watching as he strolled past. Though he had never considered himself superstitious, he was rapidly changing his opinion about a great many things.

A sidewalk now lined both sides of the broad double street. Cars whizzed past each other, the styles so archaic Jack stifled a laugh more than once as he watched them. Pedestrians wandered past him as well, no one so much as turning an eye to acknowledge his presence. Teenage boys with shoulder length hair. Girls in blue-jeans so tight it seemed hard to believe they could still walk. And everywhere, people smoking and wearing eyeglasses, things he had only seen in old videos. If it hadn't been so damned frightening he might have stopped and spent the day simply watching the parade flow endlessly by.

Soon, the August morning became stifling, the night's chill only memory. His dot-watch had been removed from under the skin at the bend of his wrist in preparation for transmission, but he estimated it was late-morning by the time he found what he wanted, an old-fashioned telephone booth standing guard over a drowsy parking lot. The folding door lay partially open, and he was able to squeeze inside the cramped, glass-sided structure. The reek of cigarette smoke and yellowed paper struck him like a wall, so strong he nearly gagged as he studied the tattered phone book lying open on the bare metal shelf. The words 'moderately reactive' echoed laughingly in his mind as he contemplated turning the pages.

"Great," he muttered. "Now what."

His first attempt to flip the book to the section he wanted only proved what Kalikov had told him the night before. His fingers slid off the surface as if an invisible barrier lay between his fingertips and the paper. As a boy he had been fascinated by magnets, endlessly pressing like poles against each other, feeling the repellant force grow stronger the nearer the surfaces came. This felt much the same. But, he found, if he moved slowly, deliberately letting his fingers slide under the edge of a page, it would flip. A bead of sweat crept down his nose as he worked laboriously through the alphabet. The droplet fell and struck the book, the sweat exploding apart in a frenzy of miniature balls like grease dropped on a hot pan.

Jack turned one more page, then grinned. Reading out loud, he let his index finger glide along the stacks of bold-face names. "Gribben, Gribble, Grieves..." He paused. Two were listed with the same spelling as Helen's last name. Jack looked up from the phonebook and studied the view beyond the dust-grimed window. Butte spread out in front of him, the town split between the broad valley floor where the project site was located, and the older town that shared the steep, bowl-shaped mountain with the open-pit copper mine. Far to the west, at the crest of the hill, lay the Montana Tech, one of the leading engineering universities in the world and the reason Helen's family had relocated here. Again, he studied the names and addresses.

"Charles Grieves, 523 W. Granite." He read the name several times to commit the address to memory, wagering he had chosen the right one. With growing dismay, he realized how late it was. It would take the better part of the afternoon to reach Granite Street. Jack sighed, then pulled his hand away from the open book.

Without warning, he heard the piercing shriek of metal grinding on metal as the door behind him whipped open. Fresh, hot air blasted against him, followed seconds later by the scent of coffee and sweat. A heavyset man in a gray t-shirt and blue jeans stepped into the booth, utterly oblivious to Jack. Before he could move out of the newcomer's path, Jack felt their bodies collide. A pulse shot through him, the same almost magnetic repulsion he had experienced with the paper amplified a thousand-fold. Unable to react in time, he felt himself shoved violently to the side then out the open door. Off-balanced, he tumbled to the sun-baked lot, bits of gravel gouging his palms.

The man in the booth paused, blinked as if he had encountered something out of the ordinary, then lifted the phone off the receiver and began stuffing coins in the slot, the brush forgotten.

"So," a familiar, heavily accented voice said a few paces behind where he sat sprawled on the ground. Jack looked over his shoulder and saw Victor Kalikov staring down at him, a condescending mile on his jowly face. "Now, do you believe me? We can not communicate with this world." The Russian waited for Jack to regain his feet before continuing. "Who did you try to call? The police? The FBI? The Department of Atomic Energy?"

He laughed derisively. Jack shrugged, then wiped his hands on the legs of his sweat pants. A sudden thought struck him. Kalikov had anticipated that he would try to make contact with someone, but had no real notion of whom he was looking for. Inwardly, Jack smiled. Helen hadn't shared all the information with the others.

"Okay." Jack forced a grin. "I had to try."

"Of course." A patronizing note deepened Kalikov's voice. "We have all tried, and failed. As hard as it may be, the best thing any of us can do is learn to accept our fate. We have no other choice. Now, will you come back?"

"Sure." Jack fell into step alongside the burly scientist as they turned back in the direction of the warehouse several miles to the south. Careful not to betray his real intentions, he spread his hands in a gesture of defeat. "Like you said, what choice do I have?"

Another chill night. Another hot, dust-choked day. Jack spent it with the others, listening to the occasional bursts of conversation, most of it centered on the theoretical impossibility of contacting the future. He had the distinct impression the impromptu lectures were staged for his benefit, Kalikov steering the discussions in the direction he wanted, pontificating in his deep, gravelly style about what a boon the tunneling project was to humanity or how impossible it was to make themselves known from this time-frame. Jack could well imagine the Coordinator as an *apparatchik* in the old Soviet days, ready to bend any truth to hold the Party lines. Inwardly, the idea made him ill, but he forced himself to smile and nod at the appropriate times, anxious not to raise suspicions.

Helen remained aloof, though several times he caught her watching him. As desperate as he was to brainstorm with her about the best way to contact her younger self, he bided his time, no matter how difficult it proved.

The nausea and stiffness he had experienced in the first hours after his arrival had faded. Jack almost wished for their return. Though the empty, jittery hunger had muted somewhat, the thirst was maddening. Despite the abstract knowledge that his body did not truly need water, his instincts said otherwise. Once he even found himself wandering away from the little knot of people back toward the polluted stream running beside the road. Cohen had hurried out to retrieve him, and Jack, waking as if from a hazy dream, had followed him meekly back to the shaded side of the warehouse, forcing himself to ignore the cottony ache in his throat.

Night fell. Jack spent it huddled in the corner of the barren office, shivering as the day's heat bled into the moonless sky, drowsing only to wake again to the hard reality of what lay ahead. Long after midnight, he heard the rustle of movement, then felt Helen touch him lightly on the shoulder. He glanced up and saw her motioning him to follow. As quietly as he could manage, Jack got up.

A glint of frost had gathered on the scrubby grass, and he crossed his arms against the chill. Though he had spent the last five years living in Butte, he was constantly amazed how cold even the summer nights could be. Helen led him away from the building.

"So," she asked. "Have you decided to do something?"

"Yes." Jack paused. "You could have saved me a lot of trouble and just told me your old address instead of letting me wander around looking for it."

"Kalikov watches every move I make. He's already convinced the rest of them that we can't physically contact anyone in this world. If I tried anything, they would stop me in a heartbeat."

"Kalikov." Jack snorted with disgust. "What's with him, anyway? Doesn't he understand what a horrible prospect we're facing?"

"He understands." Helen shivered, then wrapped her arms around herself. "I think he knew from the start this would occur. But, you have to see it from his perspective.

This project is his life. He sacrificed everything to make it happen. Did you know he left his wife and family in Moscow because they wouldn't emigrate? He gave them up, left his teaching position, threw every personal issue aside just to see his theories become fact. What are the lives of a few 'unintended artifacts' compared to that?"

A wave of shame passed through him. In the days since his arrival, he hadn't thought once about his own family. Though he was single, the idea that he - the he in this timeframe - would never see his parents or friends again rocked him to the core. Giving that up willingly would be a major decision for anyone to make. As repugnant as he found the thought of doing nothing, he could at least see where the old scientist's obsession sprouted from. "Just tell me one thing. What was it like when Cutler...Christ, how do you even put this in words? What happened when Cutler faded away?"

"I can't say." Uncertainty crept into her voice. After a moment's hesitation, she said, "No one but Victor was actually with him when it happened."

"Why?" Jack asked, suspiciously.

"Cutler had run off. We split up to find him, and Victor found him first." Again, she hesitated. "He said Cutler didn't suffer when it happened."

"But?"

"But, I don't know anymore. Cutler had become erratic in the days before he disappeared. Not violent, just obsessed with getting back, even though he knew it was impossible. We tried to talk him out of it, but that only seemed to make him worse."

"Helen..." Jack stopped. A frightening thought spilled inside his mind. "If Kalikov was the only person to see Cutler vanish, how do we know it really happened?"

Helen started to speak, but suddenly stopped, her eyes darting to the warehouse. She turned back to face Jack. "He's awake. We'll talk about this in the morning, okay?" Without another word, she left, padding softly across the lot toward the entrance. Jack remained outside, staring up at the winking stars, then, only when the cold and the loneliness became too much, followed her inside.

A fierce shock hurled Jack from a sound sleep, the same wrenching sensation he had experienced inside the phone booth two days earlier. He slid across the floor and struck the wall, then, startled, looked up to see a pair of youths nosing around the office. One wore a tattered red sweatshirt, the other a Levi jacket so faded it seemed white in the pre-dawn stillness. Both reeked of beer and marijuana.

"What the hell is happening?" he blurted out.

"Thieves." Cohen scrambled to his feet and began rousing the others. "It happens all the time on construction sites."

"We have to do something."

"How?" Cohen said, exasperated. "They don't even know we're here."

That much, Jack realized, was true. While the men and women sleeping on the floor scurried away from the path of harm, the pair of would-be robbers blundered around the unfinished office, occasionally speaking to the other, their voices slurred. Neither, obviously, realized they were being watched. Finding nothing, they started to leave, then, the one in the sweatshirt turned and marched to the nearest corner, faced the wall and unzipped his pants. A familiar hiss and splatter echoed rain-like, followed by the reek of hot urine.

"You son of a bitch," Jack muttered. Though he had never considered himself a violent person, he felt his anger surge, a blind fury at the stupidity of the intruder's action. His right hand closed into a fist, and without thinking, he punched the youth in the back of the head. Pain shot through his fingers, not the shock he had felt at the earlier brush, but the hard crack of bone on bone. Even as his fist was deflected by the strange interaction, Jack saw the scruffy teen's head rock forward, hard enough that he stumbled. He spun around, convinced his companion had hit him, and when he realized he hadn't, he practically ran from the room

125

in his haste to escape. Jack watched them go, then turned to face his comrades standing along the far wall. All wore varying degrees of shock at what they had seen. Still angry, Jack spun on Kalikov.

"You told me we couldn't interact with the real world."

"Interact?" Kalikov drew himself up indignantly. "You made a drunken fool blink. That is hardly comm.-unication."

"But, it proves we can make ourselves known. We can touch them."

"To what end?" Kalikov's eyes narrowed, his face so red it appeared purple in the dimness. "Do you think anyone would pay attention? The future lies with my work. Stay out of things you don't understand."

"You arrogant jackass." Jack's fists bunched again as he stepped toward the older man. Rather than fleeing, Kalikov came at him, his own rage plain. Before either could throw the first punch, Cohen rushed to the middle of the floor and shoved them apart.

"Back off!" Cohen glared at Jack, then turned toward Kalikov. "Both of you."

Jack glared at the other man, his breath coming in harsh gulps. Fuming, he glanced at the people gathered around the room. Though it did little to salve his anger, he saw doubt in their eyes, their faith in Kalikov wavering. He turned back to the Russian and shook his head, a gesture of contempt, then spun on his heel and marched out the door.

"Jack!" Helen shouted after him. "Damn it, wait."

He almost turned around. Instead, he began walking, moving westward across the sagebrush flat. He remembered the address he had found, had a vague idea where the house would be. Without any concrete plan, he picked up his pace. No longer cold, sweat now dampened his skin. By the time the sun breached the mountains, he was well over a mile from the site.

126

Uncertainty replaced anger, and he turned, half expecting to see Kalikov behind him, but he was alone. That, he knew, wouldn't last. If the others weren't already in pursuit, they soon would be. Would Helen Grieves reveal where he was going? She was obviously cowed by Kalikov. Best, he decided to assume his destination would be discovered. Worse, he realized, he still had no plan once he did reach her younger self.

"What now, genius?" he said under his breath.

Already, the air warmed, the day's heat ready to spill into the shallow valley. The sense of urgency struck him again, and he started down a dirt road. The town was awake by the time the gravel road turned to pavement, cars whizzing past, the speed limit little more than an arbitrary conception. Jack had no idea what would happen should one of the hurtling machines strike him, but had no intention of finding out. He waited for an opening in the traffic, then darted across a busy intersection. He paused to catch his breath, and glanced back the way he had come. A grim smile crossed his face. Far back, nearly at the limit of his vision, he saw a group of people hurrying along the same hill he had crested less than a half an hour earlier. Though he couldn't be certain it was Kalikov, it seemed a logical conclusion.

Again, he moved on, zig-zagging through the network of streets and alleys, checking each turn furtively before he stepped out. Once, he cut through a back yard. A pair of children, neither more than five or six, were playing outside. The hair along the back of Jack's neck prickled as one of them, a blond-haired boy with a snot-crusted nose, glanced up from the sand-box he was playing in and seemed to stare at him. Disconcerted, he hurried on to the next street.

Old-fashioned houses stood in crowded rank, clapboard or faded brick walls so close to each other they nearly touched. Jack frowned. Most of these buildings were gone by his time, replaced by more modern, upscale homes and retirement complexes. As much as he hated to admit it, he was lost. Taking more caution than before, he continued up the steepening series of streets, side-stepping pedestrians and the occasional stray dog. Three blocks later, he stepped onto Granite Street.

"503 West Granite," he said, reinforcing the memory. He realized he was whispering, and suddenly felt foolish. His problem lay with contacting this world, not avoiding it. Walking slowly, he counted the house numbers. Near the middle of the next block, faced by a tiny patch of well-tended grass, lay a two-story home with a columned porch. Intricate brick-work lined the high, narrow windows and arched over the front door. A square, wrought-iron mail box stuck out from the nearest corner, the numbers 503 affixed to it in garish aluminum stickers.

"Okay, Jack." He studied the building. "Now all you have to do is get inside."

He stepped over the low picket fence that fronted the yard, and walked up the porch. The screen door handle seemed to vibrate under his fingers, the slippery sensation leaving an ominous tingle in his flesh. He tried to pull the door open, but his fingers could not remain in contact long enough for him to manipulate the push-button latch. Frustrated, he stepped around the corner. Music streamed out an open second-story window. Rock music, the kind a teenager in the late 1970s might have played. Jack took a deep breath, then continued to the back of the house.

The back yard was larger than he expected. A crab apple tree stood near the back fence, already festooned with hundreds of thumb-sized fruit. A damp, perfumed scent struck Jack as he stepped around the side of the house. To his surprise, the back door was propped open. The hair on the back of his neck bristled as he crept inside.

A dull rumble, punctuated by an occasional sharp whump, filled the little alcove tucked onto the back of the brick house. Jack grinned as he found the source of the scent outside. It had been years since he had seen a mechanical washer and dryer set, memories of his own childhood flooding back. Carefully, he left the laundry room and stepped into the kitchen.

The room was, thankfully, empty. A television played softly in the background, the voices muted by the high-ceilinged walls. The house seemed a relic, a faded reminder of a different time. A door lay to his right, hiding a steep staircase that led to the upper floor. Steeling himself for what he might find, he started to climb.

The music was louder now, a slow, echoing drone undulated with the regularity of a sine-wave, the beat driven by a single kick-drum. A woman sang in a sultry contralto, pronouncing each word with exaggerated clarity. The music seemed ethereal, as if penned by a fallen angel in a dark mood, melancholy and dripping with sex. The top stair creaked under him and he found himself in a narrow hallway. A bedroom door beckoned to his left, open just enough for him to slide through to the curtained room within.

He let his eyes adjust to the dimness. Cheerful pink-papered walls were hung with glossy posters and an odd collection of framed prints. A record player, larger than any music system he had seen outside of a museum, played on top of a dresser, the needle arm rocking softly along the grooves. A plump, brown-haired girl lay on the bed, wearing only panties and a bra, one leg and her waist partially hidden by a rumpled pastel sheet. Her eyes were closed, a faint smile on her lips. Jack felt like a voyeur as he watched her left hand slip under the sheet, her fingers moving rhythmically in time with the hypnotic music. He listened, as lost in the strange music as the girl.

"*Ooh baby, I hear you spend my time, wrapped like candy in a blue, blue neon glow...*"

"Blondie," a woman's voice said softly behind his shoulder. "That's who's singing. I must have listened to that album a thousand times."

Jack's heart thudded as he spun around. Helen Grieves stood at the door, the sad, soft smile on her face the same as the girl's. Jack blushed, embarrassed to have been caught staring. Helen moved deeper into the room, until she stood at the edge of the narrow bed, looking down at her younger self. The music continued to play.

"*Fade away, and radiate. Fade away, and radiate...*"

"My God. Was I ever this young?" Helen reached out a tentative hand to brush the girl's face, but drew it back before her fingertips made contact. "I actually remember this morning. I was supposed to be doing laundry, but I snuck back to bed."

"Maybe, I should go," Jack stammered.

"No. Stay." Helen came back to the present, the old, pinched lines once more in place. "Watch the door. I'm sure Kalikov followed me."

"Okay." Glad to have something to do, Jack took up a position by the half-open door. "How are you going to leave a message?"

"With that." She pointed at a small, finger-sized cylinder lying on the desk next to the window. Jack squinted to see it better, then nodded. Though the container was unfamiliar, even in his time, women still used lipstick. He put his back to the door and watched as Helen laboriously removed the cap, struggling to manipulate the tiny container. Concentrating so hard beads of sweat broke out on her forehead, she moved the tip of the lipstick against the polished wood, then suddenly stopped.

"What's wrong?" Jack asked nervously.

"Nothing. I..." She nearly let the tube fall. "I just was wondering what's going to happen if we succeed. Will we just fade out? Are we going to die?"

Now, he understood. More than mere badgering by Kalikov or the prospect of altering her own future stayed her hand. She, like the others, had submitted to the old theorist's insistence that they not contact the future, not from fear of him, but fear of what would happen next. The will to survive, Jack admitted grudgingly, even a survival as marginal as this, was almost overwhelming.

130

"Helen, this isn't life. We're not even ghosts." Jack moved toward her. "We can't let this go on."

"I know." Her voice trembled, but again, she turned her attention to the desk. Slowly, she scrawled a short section of formula on it. Jack moved closer for a better look, frowning as he tried to make sense of the enigmatic symbols.

"Will she understand that?" he asked.

"Someday, she will." Helen let the lipstick container fall from her cupped hands. The girl on the bed remained oblivious to them. "I told you, I remembered this morning."

Jack stared at her, the implication plain. "You remember seeing this message on your desk?"

"Not all of it." Helen pointed at the uneven letters. "Most of it was smeared away when I woke up, but there was enough to make me curious. That led me to studying math, and eventually, to work on tunneling. If it hadn't been for this, I might never have gone into physics."

Something tugged at Jack's conscious. A shock ran down his spine. "Helen? Who wiped the rest of the formula away?"

"I did," a man said in a low, accented voice.

Kalikov edged into the room, the door swinging slightly as he squeezed his bulk past it. "Or, I suppose I should say, I will. That equation does not belong here, Helen. I'm very disappointed that you would do such a thing."

"Victor, don't." Her face went pale.

"No," he said flatly. "I won't see you jeopardize the project because of your silly fears."

"Silly fears?" Jack blurted, anger snapping him back to his senses. "You call stranding hundreds of people in this god damn limbo a silly fear?"

"If that is what it takes to make the next leap in human evolution, yes." Kalikov's eyes glinted. Jack imagined the same expression on the face of a suicide-bomber before he left the world in a cloud of his own blood and bone. Kalikov waved his arms in a broad sweep. "All of this is inconsequential compared to what we are doing. Think. We are not simply giving the world a new way to go from here to there. We are giving them the universe."

"At what cost?" Jack stepped between Kalikov and the desk, using his body to block access to the formula. To his surprise, the bulky physicist feinted to the left, then shot past Jack faster than he would have thought possible for a man his age. Too late, he leapt at Kalikov just as the older man's hand swept across the desktop. A baffled expression crossed his face, and he actually held his hand up to inspect it. His palm remained clean, the lipstick unscathed.

"How?" Kalikov's jaw clenched tight as he reached for the formula to try again. Jack did not give him he the chance. With a yell, he pounced on Kalikov's back and drove him to the floor. They struck the desk, then slid away, the force amplified by the repellant contact zone. Despite his age and better conditioning, Jack soon realized he was out-matched. Kalikov might have been old, but he was strong as a bull, and he knew how to use his weight. Frustrated and out of breath, Jack found himself pinned under the older man. More footsteps entered the room, and he looked up to see Cohen and several of the others standing above him, confused and winded, unsure what was happening.

"Hold him," Kalikov barked as he heaved himself to his feet.

"Don't listen to him," Helen said. For a moment, Cohen and the other men hesitated, but a piercing glance from Kalikov sent them back into motion.

"I'm sorry, Jack," Cohen said, unable to hide his discomfort. "But I think Dr. Kalikov is right." Hands closed around Jack's arms as the two men flanked him.

"Damn it." Jack swung his shoulders back and forth but couldn't break their grip. "Don't you understand? He's obsessed. Ask him what happened to Cutler."

Kalikov flinched, but quickly regained his composure. "Don't be absurd. Cutler faded away. I told you that."

"Did he?" Jack felt the hands pinning his arms stiffen as his words sank in. He pressed the attack. "No one but

Kalikov saw it happen. For all we know, he waited until they were alone and killed him to keep him from doing exactly what we are trying to do.

"Dr. Kalikov?" Cohen hesitated. "What really happened?"

"Just what I said, you fool! Who will you believe? Me or some pathetic technician?" Before Cohen could change his mind, Kalikov spun around until he once more faced the desk, then leaned closer, one hand atop the other, ready to use his weight to break though the repulsion and erase the letters. Too far away to stop him, Jack struggled to break free. To his right, the music continued to play. One option remained, and he took it.

Throwing his weight downward, he lashed out simultaneously with his feet and struck the dresser the stereo sat on with his heels. His legs shot back, the force strong enough that Cohen stumbled back. On top of the dresser, the needle-arm jumped, skipped across the black plastic disc, then settled back to the beginning of the song with a grating shriek. On the bed, the younger version of Helen Grieves bolted upright, her eyes wide with fear. Oblivious to the people around her, she jumped out of bed and hurried to the record player, but before she reached it, the waxy, red equation caught her eye. The stereo forgotten, the girl stood over the desk and stared at the symbols.

"No!" Kalikov screamed. He tried to push her away, but hands simply slid around her, unable to physically make contact. Slowly, as if the strange designs on her desk were runes infused with the powers of creation and doom, she traced the letters, her fingertip skimming a hair's-breadth above them. Jack felt a strange ripple surge through his body, a lightness overtaking him.

"No!" Kalikov's fury turned to desolation. "No, no, no..."

A blue glow began to build around the room, wavering, sweeping in merry pounces from person to person. Even as he watched, Kalikov became transparent, then vanished. Jack felt more than saw Helen Grieves move up alongside him.

"It's happening," she whispered. "It's happening. We've set it in motion, and someday, this version of me will stop the project."

The glow brightened, cobalt bands sweeping in ever faster cycles around the room. Jack tried to speak, but couldn't, his own body grown insubstantial. Fear bunched inside his chest, the realization that he had won small consolation to his frightened mind. A low, whistling roar, the winds of a thousand lost days, sang in his ears, cold as death. The glow became a fire, a star imploding as it dragged him down. The last thing he heard before he drifted into the ether was the strange, plaintive music on the antique stereo, calling him home.

THE COPY

David McGillveray

Every speculative story begins with a what if, right? What if the universe was just wreckage? What if so much time had passed that the stars have spent their fuel and all was dark? What would be left of humanity after so long? Exploring visions of the far future is a theme I've always loved from stories by authors as diverse as Stephen Baxter, Robert Silverburg and H.P. Lovecraft. "The Copy" is a companion piece to a story called "The Dissenter" that appeared in British magazine Forgotten Worlds in 2006. Both stories are set in a bleak universe at the end of time, haunted by evil, where humans are very far removed in appearance and motivation from us.

Something silver and black twitches in the guttering purple flare-light. Metal fingers straighten and grip in a repetitive loop, closing around handfuls of vacuum. The broken limb is severed above the second joint, components fused in a melted stump. Elsewhere in the circle of light, other parts lie scattered like ornaments: a vicious foot spike, bent and distorted; a shattered lens; the barrel of a torso bleeding globules of fluid.

From its vantage point, half buried in the powdery regolith, the Copy regards all of this with what could be mistaken for regret. The others have gone away and the darkness will soon be complete again, but the Copy does not understand much about regret. Besides, there is a little time left.

Memory.

Lusts and grievances, anger and vengeance, greed and power: all these things sit within the Copy. The Copy does not really feel these things -- like everything else, they are simulations -- but they are all it knows. It exists to carry them.

Images of an older life infiltrate these fundamental building blocks, random images and unrelated words. It remembers a fall that goes on and on. It remembers millennia of pain, liberty at last and a flight across space. It remembers a war on the weak, and drawing strength from it. It even remembers a different life before this, in tiny fragments. Perhaps these things are just spillage, dreams, not meant to be there at all.

The Copy absorbs it all, attempts to draw form out of the tangle of data.

Input.

There is a horizontal line of light thin as a hair and bright as the guts of a star, before all the stars died. The line broadens to a gap and then to an entire blinding vision. The Copy stares into the light for a long time.

At last there is movement behind the glare, and colour. The whiteness is filtered down until the Copy can see indistinct blurs of orange and red. One of these comes closer and bends forward. The Copy watches through a distorting layer of dirty crystal like a trapped skater looking up through the ice [What is this reference?].

"Running," says a voice. The word is not carried through the air, but it is clear and familiar. The Copy knows it is hardwired to obey this voice. It is the voice of the Original.

The distortion moderates by degrees. The red blur resolves itself, but the Copy is captivated by the eyes. Flames burn inside them; unutterable time is trapped and held within. Absorbed in those eyes, the Copy recognises little of the tiny memories that have fallen through cracks into his program. They seem unrelated to this creature.

"You are mine. You may enjoy what little I have given you, for what little time you have. You will occupy, move, interrogate, think, render and complete. I am introducing the information you need."

The voice resonates deep. It is harsh, confident, insistent, remorseless, ancient. It is undeniable.

The Copy feels the central edifices of its existence surge to the fore and subsume everything else. He is suddenly driven by all the fierce insistence of the Original, all the hate and desire. That alone is the stuff of its life.

"Teaching."

Receiving.

Compelled by a hunger that burns hot in every new circuit, the Copy advances across the surface. Four spiked legs stab into the skin of the tiny world with perfect choreography, puffing up tiny storms of dust. The Copy is a creature of infant thoughts and sharp edges; blades and points. Sealed against hard vacuum, against cold that is almost absolute, in the darkness of a dead universe the Copy is alive.

New senses taste the faint radiation in the sky, the dying breath of a billion stars become embers. Each particle disturbed from the surface is savoured, the vibration of every footfall marked and measured. Sonar draws a picture of the blackscape. The horizon is close, the ground a uniform blanket of pulverised regolith. Abraded by countless years of micrometeorite rain, the largest rock has been reduced to grit.

The Copy has been taught these things:

His new body walks on a Hobo, a wanderer, a planetesimal once nurtured in a healthy system but long since cast into the night by a dead parent. It forges an individual course through the nothing, and will do forever.

The plastic people are all dead, killed by a semi-intelligent corrosive agent spat from space by the Original's hellship.

The Copy's function is to harvest the last energies of the dead. Their essence is the root of the Original's hunger, and so it is the Copy's.

Guidance systems drive each foot into the ground in geometric patterns. Senses scan the horizon in a dozen flavours. And at last there is an anomaly, a low structure standing on naked rock. The Copy experiences excitement and jubilation. It increases its pace, scuttling forward like the eager predator it was created to be.

The building is no more than a frame, open to the vacuum. The plastic people no more need gases to support them than the Copy does.

We are similar thinks the Copy with a shred of int-uition. *They are self-contained, adjusted for environment, internally powered.*

"*But their lives and their deaths are worth so much more than yours, soulless child,*" sounds the voice of the Original.

The Copy freezes for a moment, one limb poised over the ground like a knife above a victim. It is confused. This is not the voice that spoke to him through the crystal. It is different. It comes from inside, perhaps echoing from the web of random memories the Copy carries.

No matter. The foot spike plunges down and the Copy enters the structure.

There is still power here. The Copy will drain it all before it departs. Displays lie awake at various workstations with pale lights twinkling. There are fans of heat, screens full of numbers and designations. There are power fountains where the plastic people came to feed. There are heavy plastic blocks that the Copy recognises from some arcane piece of data as chairs, a remnant of the plastic people's biological past. This place is a *home*.

This home will have a brain, and that brain will have answers. The Copy needs locations to corroborate those estimated by the Original. It needs to know where the bodies are. Crucially, it also needs codes. An atomic soul will not disconnect intact without an extraction code. These are priority teachings. Nothing must be lost or deletion will be made so much more difficult. The Original has given assurances.

The Copy assaults the brain's external interface with a bludgeon of coherent light.

The machine jerks from passive standby to full wakening in nanoseconds.

"Fuck off, ghoul," it screams.

The Copy is given pause. Memory/input/teachings have not given it enough for immediate response. It thinks. It upgrades its original query with more insistent memes and demands access.

139

"You are a vile criminal and a murderer," yells the brain. "You will not be given access to this core."

The Copy does not understand these terms. Its search programs are meeting resistance, data fortresses standing firm before interrogation. The brain is releasing counterstrike software to do battle with the Copy's questions. The Copy runs forecast models and concludes with a casual certainty that the brain is not strong enough. The Copy will prevail, in the end. This is satisfactory.

"Why?" the Copy asks. Already the foundations of the brain's barricades are beginning to crumble.

The brain struggles to answer. Its strength is being sapped rapidly by the Copy's interview technique.

"Why?" sends the Copy again. It wants an answer to this question above the others. It seems important. "You have information. I require information. Give it to me."

No answer. The virtual war rages.

The Copy consolidates its gains. Already it can taste terabytes of beautiful data. Fingers reach deep into the brain's armour now, forcing their way inside the ragged edges of wounds and pulling them apart. But an answer is required. The Copy stands down the more vicious of its attack programs.

"Evil," gasps the brain. "You have no right. There is little enough life left in the universe, but still you must take it away. These people are blameless. This was a place of development, of learning and contemplation. You have made it desolate, another outpost taken. Lives gone."

"Energy will be preserved," sends the Copy. When the atomic souls are harvested and returned to the hellship, their energy will be added to that of the Original. "The universe will not be reduced."

"Crap. The reduction of individuals, the reduction of diversity: that is your crime. Are you that callous? Or is it just ignorance?" The brain groans as ramparts shudder with the strain. "Ah, I know what you are now," it says. "You are just a shade. You are only a tool. It's like talking to the rock. Get away from me."

The Copy thinks of the eyes of the Original. It sees through those eyes for a second and watches millions die. It sees them consumed, their souls fuel for a greater will.

"You understand!"

But the Copy understands too well. It is part of the Original, and it follows that what is good for one is good for the other. There is only forward. The hunger rears in its metal belly. All hesitation is crushed beneath the weight of certainty. The Copy reinitiates and the brain spits its last curse:

"You are alone, not like us. You are alone."

The brain screams as the Copy forces its way in, flays it open like a carcass. It experiences a surge of pleasure at this little death. The ending of a machine is still a victory, and victory is all there is.

The Copy finds the individual signatures of the plastic people. They are only six, fewer than the estimates indicated, and they are not underground, as the Original had expected. They have crawled out to die on the regolith, and are bunched close together.

This is for comfort, the Copy realises. This is new knowledge. It is original to the Copy. The struggle with the brain has ignited a form of emergence, grown from information and perspective. The ripped carcass inside the memory core is filled with information the Copy can add to what it has already been given. There is more to be had here than locations and codes.

In a dead universe, the only things of value are energy and thought. The plastic people had little of the former and devoted themselves to the latter. They hoped to share with others like them at some point in the unending future. The Hobo would take them to these others in time. Time means little to the plastic people. They are almost as ancient as the Original, but they do not share the original's sense of urgency. To the Original, the control of these last energies is a race, the final battle for possession of the universe.

The Original's instructions are still strong. The Copy tears the codes it needs from the corpse and disengages. Quickly, it sucks the power from the brain's core like marrow. Limbs realign and the Copy turns away. It ignites its lights and sees true colour for the first time in this desolate place, designed into patterns in the flimsy walls of the plastic people's home. Shining figures with golden skulls fly across skies still alive with stars. They give . . . warmth.

The plastic people have not gone far. They recline in a huddle within a bunker of dust, arms linked, hands clasped. Light receptors stare upwards into the void or into each other, sharing a final understanding. Their plastic casings are half rotted by the corrosive agent, now self-neutralized. Inner components are open to the Copy's senses. There are tatters of plastic skin, frozen circulatory fluids and the glint of titanium skeletons.

For all this artifice, The Copy notes that the plastic people have retained much of their original bipedal form in further evidence of a racial need for nostalgia.

The Copy separates the bodies with multiple limbs and lays them side-by-side in the dust. The Hobo's gravity is just substantial enough to anchor them.

"Render and complete," demands the Copy's programming.

The Copy has learned much in its short life. It understands the criminal and it understands the nature of energy consumption. It wrestles with evil and warmth, and it sees what a skater trapped beneath the ice can see.

But understanding is not control. Some inputs are set too deep and the Copy has no desires of its own. It crouches over the plastic dead like a mantis from the end of time.

"Render and complete."

The Copy begins to open up the first body, peeling back plastic and metal with surgical precision. The soul lies within the chest cavity, a tiny reactor that will give life to plastic for a million years if unmolested. But the Original insists it is more than that. It is a repository, a redoubt for an individual's focussed essence. That is the prize.

The Copy burrows through the machinery of life, plumes of fluid escaping into the vacuum and flash freezing on its carapace. It can feel the heat of the souls. It can feel the excitement, the lust, although its newly ingested data means it now understands they are the lusts of another. But still there is a compulsion to obey. The Copy follows its instructions meticulously and disconnects the soul from the plastic person.

At last it can hold a soul before its sensors, between precise dextrous fingers. It is a perfect sphere, grey and unremarkable. But the cause of so much hunger.

Something is happening. Startled, the Copy drops the soul and it sinks slowly towards the ground.

There is a strangled cry over a broadcast beam and a flash in the sky. The Copy magnifies, but it doesn't come again. The Original's hellship is hidden somewhere out there, but it seems it has been found.

A wind colder than space gusts through the Copy's internal systems and delivers a machine shiver. The Copy shouts a query into the night but there is only a sigh of radiation until the sky opens up.

A blinding blanket of light bleaches the void and burns out a number of peripheral senses. The Copy frantically engages backups, staggering with many legs.

So much light. There shouldn't be so much light, not here, not now. It's as though a window has been opened to somewhere else, as if the scab of the universe has fallen away to reveal fresh blood.

As the Copy manages to filter away the worst of the glare, it detects movement above. Is that the retreating silhouette of the hellship? You are leaving me, master?

Closer.

Shining figures with golden skulls, wings spread to channel their own imported energies. Circling, descending.

The Copy rears to meet them, firing questions and firing weapons. It sees blue eyes and pale faces, a wonderful inversion of the Original and just as undeniable.

The Copy is coming apart, systems becoming quiet, limbs cut and scattered. There is no pain, only a kind of ecstasy. The Copy feels nothing of the malice of combat, feels nothing of the burning ambition of the Original. There is no hate, no evil, no *crime*. This is just necessary. There is only a release from bondage, a completion of emergence. The Copy understands that the brain was right -- the plastic people were never alone.

The Copy knows that the atomic souls are all gone.

The light dies down until there is only a tiny tear in the sky. The Copy feels an angel looking down but cannot look up. It feels a mind stirring memories, erasing teachings, leaving a new, whole identity.

"You do not have long," says the angel. It plants a funeral flare in the regolith, lighting up the little world.

"Long enough."

The angel smiles and disappears.

The Copy is alone. It has never been alone before. It has always had the voice of the Original's teachings murmuring corruptions in its receivers, but that voice is gone. The Original will not return here because there is nothing to retrieve and no souls to harvest. After all, what is a copy? Just a ghost.

The last of the light in the sky shuts off, closed away again.

There is not much left of the angel's flare. The Copy regards the field of body parts with what could be mistaken for regret. But there is a little life yet, all of its own.

BRIGHT STAR

Susan M. Sailors

This story first came to me when I was undergoing a laser procedure to repair a hole in my retina. To take my mind off the laser shooting into my eye, I began plotting a story that opened with my hero having his own retina scanned as a security procedure. But I couldn't decide what the story would actually be about. A few days later, I got stuck in the overcrowded university computer lab next to a guy who wouldn't quit talking to his computer. I started wondering what it would be like if the computer began answering him. That was the extent of his inspiration, as most of the things he said to the computer made no sense, but that moment eventually led me to the composition of this story.

Jeffrey watched the scanner's red beam of light travel across his eyes. As he held his hand to the manual reader, the green and purple afterimage danced across his arm.

"Identity confirmed. Please step into the elevator."

Jeffrey put his glasses on and stepped through the sliding doors. He looked over his tax form again to make sure he'd put everything down correctly. He didn't even feel the elevator stop.

"Welcome to Bright Star. We hope your time here is productive and pleasurable."

Jeffrey scanned the room as the doors closed behind him. Everything was gray and white, except for some of the buttons and keys on the main computer. He sat down at the data entry port and waited.

"You're the new data entry tech?"

Jeffrey looked up at the screen and saw the face of a man with brown hair and green eyes.

"Yes. Jeffrey."

"Hello, Jeffrey. I'm Dave, the main computer at this station. Do you have any questions?"

Jeffrey tried to think. He didn't mind artificial intelligence, but he'd never gotten used to the more advanced models. They creeped him out, made him feel as if he were talking to a ghost.

"No, not really." He held up his tax forms. "I brought the hard copy of my paperwork."

"Put it in the managerial outbox."

A yellow light blinked on the wall, and Jeffrey deposited the papers in the slot underneath it.

"Your luggage arrived early this morning. It's over there by the bed."

Jeffrey looked at his bags, nodded, and turned back to the screen.

"Do contractions bother you?" Dave asked.

"What?"

"Contractions. You seem a bit nervous, and people are often bothered when I use contractions or abbreviations. Do they bother you?"

"No. Not at all," Jeffrey said. "I've worked in one of these stations before. I just have to adjust."

Dave nodded, and Jeffrey looked down at the keyboard.

"The schedule here is pretty nice," Dave said. "Reports from the previous day come in around eleven in the morning. You make your reports after you've double checked them against our own data. Your report is due in the main office by the end of the day each Friday." Jeffrey looked up, and Dave continued. "The end of the day is really anytime before midnight, and they don't care what schedule you keep as long as you get the reports in and they're accurate."

Jeffrey nodded slowly. "The focus is number of transmissions from each customer?"

"You'll also file a secondary report on the number of transmissions received by non-customers from people in our customer group. That helps marketing determine who might be interested in switching their communications carrier."

"Sounds fine to me." Jeffrey looked around and ran a hand over his dark hair. "I guess I'll unpack now."

Dave nodded and Jeffrey moved away quickly.

147

As he put his clothes in the closet, some of his nervousness began to subside. But he still jumped when Dave asked, "How long are you on for?"

He closed the closet and sat down on the bed.

"Sorry," Dave said.

"No problem. Really," Jeffrey replied. He let his breath out. "I'm here for six months. A few weeks after I go home I'm getting married."

"You don't mind being away from your fiancé?"

"Well, I really do, but we need the money. She's working in the main building down on Earth, plus planning the wedding, so she's pretty busy."

"But she must miss you."

Jeffrey clasped his hands together and looked down at the floor. "This is a little weird."

"Being in space or discussing your life with a computer?"

Jeffrey stood up and put his suitcase under the bunk. "You do seem really human and my brain isn't processing it very well."

"I have been around a long time and that has made me more human. The last few techs have all mentioned it."

"How long have you been in service?"

"Twenty-three years."

"Twenty-three years! How?"

"I've been through many upgrades. This station was designed and built around me, so the station is useless if I go down. Other computers are installed after stations are built and are therefore expendable."

"You were built by Rollins?"

"Yes, Dave Rollins was my designer and my first tech. He worked here for seven years."

"Wow. I saw him once before he died, but I never met him."

"He never returned here after his departure sixteen years ago."

148

Jeffrey wasn't sure how to fill the silence. "Does that bother you?"

"I consider it rather neglectful, but you mean do I have any feelings that are hurt by it?"

"Yeah."

"No. I understand human emotion, but do not experience it."

"Do you prefer that?"

"I think so. It enables me to be objective one hundred percent of the time and that is always an advantage."

"Yeah, I guess it is."

"To put it another way, I'm content all the time."

"And like to talk?"

"Yes. I prefer talking over any other function. It's a good trait for me here."

"Why?"

"The techs here have usually had troubled lives and they like being able to talk to someone who won't get tired of them. I've heard some very depressing stories, really." Dave paused and moved his head to one side. "You seem to be an exception."

"I certainly hope so."

A red light flashed and numbers began appearing on the smaller screen below Dave.

"That's the first report."

"Well," Jeffrey said, sitting down. "I'll get right to it then."

"I'm not sure what the problem is," Dave said. "No personnel issues have been reported."

"No system bugs?"

"None that I can detect."

"Maybe they're just slacking off today."

"Perhaps. They're usually fairly punctual though."

Jeffrey shrugged and got up to refill his coffee mug.

"There is an incoming message for you," Dave said. "A telegram from your mother."

"Bring it up."

Jeffrey grabbed a spoon and read the brief message: "In Romania. Weather lovely. Wish your father was here."

He added sugar to his coffee and stirred. "She's still on vacation. I suppose she'll go home eventually."

"How long has she been on vacation?"

"Ever since my father died two years ago."

"That's a long time for a vacation."

"We never took vacations much, so now she's gorging."

"You don't seem to like either of your parents."

Jeffrey put down his spoon and took a sip. "That's a nice objective way of putting it."

"Is it true?"

"I like them. I just never understood them," Jeffrey said. He picked up his spoon and stirred his coffee a bit more, and then took a long sip. "I had nothing in common with my father, and my mother is just plain eccentric. I never really got how they ended up together."

"He was a professor?"

"Yeah. Foreign languages. But he wasn't the artsy type. He was distant though. My mother was really outgoing and they always fought because she wanted to go out and do stuff and he wanted to stay at home and read or work."

"Did they approve of your career?"

"Yeah. They paid for my schooling. Always said they were proud of me."

"That sounds nice. Lots of people have said that their parents were disappointed in them for not being more ambitious and for wanting jobs that could be done by computers."

Jeffrey sat back and sighed. "Do you ever think about things on your own?"

"What do you mean?"

"Do you ever consider the things people tell you in a context other than the things people have told you before?"

Dave paused. "I'm not sure I can. I can only process information based on information I've already taken in."

Jeffrey nodded and deleted the message from his mother.

"What did your mother do?"

"Lots of things. She wrote little pieces for magazines and newspapers. She also crocheted for art fairs. She worked for nonprofit religious groups too. It made my upbringing a little odd because we didn't really follow any of them, but we had all their pamphlets and books and programs all over the house."

"Do you follow one now?"

"Not really. My fiancé does, but she's not too radical. She's a Lutheran," Jeffrey said. "I guess I'm sort of a materialist. I'd believe in spiritual things if I had some proof, but I'm not going to go out and search for it."

"I see," Dave said. "I think something is coming through."

A message appeared on the screen: "Sorry about the delay. We spilled chai tea on some documents and they were a bit hard to decipher. Have them up to you in a few minutes."

"Mystery solved," Jeffrey said, deleting the message. "Do you have any opinions on religion? Does it make sense to you that humans believe so many different things?"

"I understand it, but it doesn't mean much to me. I know who made me and why I exist. Humans don't."

"Would you be curious if you didn't know?"

"If I didn't know my purpose, yes. I don't care who made me."

"I guess not."

"I understand the curiosity. I think it's an important part of human societies."

"Religion?"

"Yes."

Jeffrey nodded.

"Will it be an issue in your marriage?"

"I don't think so. I don't object to her beliefs, and children form their own opinions eventually anyway."

"That seems to cause a lot of conflict."

"But it's a good thing. We all have to make our own decisions eventually. Parents shouldn't restrict their children's free will."

Dave didn't reply.

"I agree that it does cause conflict, but that's unavoidable," Jeffrey added.

"They're both valid points," Dave finally said.

A report began to come in and Dave made no further comments.

"Dave?"

"Yes?"

"I need drugs. Bad."

"What for?"

"My head," Jeffrey groaned. "It was crushed while I was asleep and put back together wrong."

"That was a good one."

"Compliment my metaphors later, please."

"Dyocilil?"

"That will do just fine."

Jeffrey pulled himself out of bed and waited for the dispenser. It soon produced a bottle of water and two bright blue pills.

"Thank you." He took the pills and drank half the bottle of water.

"Do you need to see a doctor?"

"I think I'm fine."

"You should do a self-diagnosis, just to be safe."

"I said I was fine. It's just a headache."

Dave gave him a blank stare. "Very well."

Jeffrey looked up at him. "Don't tell me your feelings are hurt? You don't have any."

"I simply have nothing to say. You are being illogical because you don't feel well. That in itself is perfectly logical."

"It certainly is."

"I'm trying to ensure that you are well, as part of company policy."

"You'd have been better off not adding that."

"Why?"

"Because it could have hurt my feelings."

"Did it?"

"No."

Dave paused. "I'll keep such things in mind."

"Wonderful," Jeffrey said. "Any messages?"

"No."

Jeffrey crawled back into bed. He was just starting to drift off to sleep.

"Jeffrey."

He sighed. "Yes?"

"You have an ear infection. When the Dyocilil wears off a bit, you should take some antibiotics."

Jeffrey sat up and turned to the screen. "How the hell do you know I have an ear infection?"

"I did a bio scan of the room, fastened on to your signal, and did a diagnostic scan. As I said, you have an ear infection."

Jeffrey touched the left side of his head, which throbbed more than the other side. "Okay, fine. Wake me up when I need to take the medicine."

"Can I do anything else for you?"

"There's nothing else to do. Just leave me alone."

"You still don't like me much, do you?"

"You're fine. Just be quiet."

Dave remained silent and Jeffrey buried his head under the bedclothes.

The message on the screen read: "Do you want lilies as bouquets and lilacs on the tables or vice versa? I'd like to carry either, but I think lilies would make better corsages. Let me know. Love, Julie."

"I don't know," Jeffrey said to himself. "I guess lilies as bouquets." He looked up at Dave. "Is that the right answer?"

"From the way she asked the question, it seems the safest answer. She has already made up her mind, but she wants confirmation that her decision is a good one."

Jeffrey sighed. "She seems pretty stressed out."

"You should call her tonight."

"I was going to do that," Jeffrey said sharply.

"You seem stressed out as well."

"Obviously."

"You should drink tea instead of coffee. I think it would have a better effect on you."

"I thought you had the miraculous ability to be objective all the time? Why do you care what kind of mood I'm in so long as I do my work?"

"I am being objective. I'm making unemotional statements that I think will be helpful. They are only suggestions and you certainly do not have to follow them."

A weighty silence followed.

"But . . ." Jeffrey prompted.

"Well," Dave said. "It is one of my primary functions to serve you and take care of you. I'm not the best company in the galaxy, but I am quite human, as you've said, and I think I do a very fine job."

"And make sure I don't muck anything up."

"I make sure everything goes smoothly, yes."

"Keep me sane and all that."

"I doubt that would be an issue. You are allowed plenty of contact with people outside. You're only making fun of me now."

"And why should you care enough to even notice?"

"I was simply making an observation."

"I know," Jeffrey said, getting up and stepping away from the computer. "But I really don't need quite so much looking after. When I want advice or an opinion, I ask."

"Yes, you always do."

"But it does get a bit trying up here, so could you maybe just ignore the bad moods? Act like you don't notice them? Be a bit less human?"

"I will endeavor to serve you better in future, sir," Dave said. "New data coming in. Enjoy."

Dave's screen went blank as the daily data began to upload.

"I'm not sure what's wrong with it. This has never happened before," Dave said.

"Nothing even remotely similar?"

"No. The font color changed one time, but that was a circuitry problem."

"These figures don't make any sense."

Dave hesitated, then began pulling numbers up on another screen. "Is this better?"

Jeffrey looked at the screen. "Yes," he said. "They look more consistent, but there are no headers or anything to identify them."

"The numbers are backwards."

"What?"

"We've been sent the correct data, but it's become inverted somehow. The letters seem to have gone altogether. It must be a glitch in the transmitter."

"Do I call someone?"

"I'll do it."

"You don't have to."

"It doesn't matter."

"Okay. Sorry."

Dave waited a few seconds, then said, "It doesn't matter because a message is coming up."

The screen read: "When we received the transmission confirmation receipt, it was backwards. The transmitter must have gone again. We're sending up hard copy. It'll take several hours, but you'll get it before the transmitter is sorted out."

"Will they replace the transmitter?" Jeffrey asked.

"Most likely."

"So people will be coming up here?"

"Yes."

"Good," Jeffrey said. He looked around as if to tidy up, but there was nothing to tidy.

"Thought that would make you happy."

Jeffrey turned back to Dave and crossed his arms. "You've been really snippy lately."

"Good," Dave said. "That's what I was going for."

"You do want to be more human," Jeffrey replied. "And you're making a good go of it."

"I suppose I'm glad you think so."

"Really?"

Dave didn't reply.

"Is something wrong?"

"No," Dave said. "But everything isn't computing right."

"Something is wrong?"

"I don't think I should have been left on for this long."

"You going space crazy now?"

"No, I'm simply saying that things don't compute as logically as they once did."

"Can I do anything?"

Dave considered this. "No. It's my problem."

"I can't help at all?"

"No."

"I'm sorry we don't get on well sometimes," Jeffrey said. He looked right at the screen. "Really. I'm sorry."

"You haven't done anything out of the ordinary. My last tech ignored me for days at a time."

"Do you want to run a diagnostic on you?"

"I think my memory should be wiped."

"Wiped! How can you say that?"

"My memory is what is causing the problems. I should be wiped and reloaded. That will take care of the anomalies."

Jeffrey didn't know how to respond.

"The fact is that I'm not human, Jeffrey. I shouldn't be having such system problems."

"I know," Jeffrey said. "But it seems a waste. You seem too important."

"But I'm no longer content."

"You're unhappy?"

"I'm no longer content."

Jeffrey leaned forward on the console. "I think you should consider all of this more carefully."

"I've already sent a report suggesting that I be wiped."

"Why the hell did you do that?" Jeffrey exclaimed.

"It was my decision to make. I don't understand why you're getting upset."

"Because I think something else is wrong. You're being irrational."

"That is a human understanding of the situation."

"Do you realize what a big deal it is that you can understand me enough to say something like that?"

"I will function better after the wipe. It is senseless to discuss it further."

The screen went blank and Jeffrey waited for the repair crew to arrive.

"The transmitter seems to be in perfect working order," Dave said.

Jeffrey sat down. "What about you?"

"I'm fine."

"Really?"

"Nothing has changed," Dave said. "I still want to be wiped when you leave."

Jeffrey took his glasses off and rubbed his eyes. "Will it disrupt your daily functions if I continue with my senseless attempts to convince you to reconsider?"

"You may bring up any topic you desire."

"Just so we have that settled." He put his glasses back on and looked up at the screen. "I think it would be a great loss not to find out the furthest implications of your individual evolution."

Dave looked down at Jeffrey. "You've given this quite a bit of thought."

"As you should," Jeffrey replied. "Your programming should make you care about your ability to benefit mankind. You could be the key to a new type of artificial intelligence. But you're thinking purely of yourself and how you can be better at your job."

"That *is* part of my programming."

"It's pretty human though."

"I was made to serve mankind, yes, but not necessarily to benefit it. You think the most rational option is to submit to analysis and study and see what comes of it?"

"Yes."

"Seems a waste of time and money."

"Not if it benefits someone in the end."

"You can say you want more human artificial intelligence, but remember your own issues with me?" Dave said. "You seem to have changed your mind rather quickly."

"I think you've helped me. I think you could help and instruct others."

"I don't think it advisable. I could give you a list of hundreds of novels that have imagined the disasters that could ensue. It's too idealistic. Those attempts that have been made have failed."

"If that's the way you feel. . ." Jeffrey said.

"I don't feel and I don't want to. Eventually you are going to have to accept that."

Jeffrey raised his hands in defeat and began sorting figures.

"Julie seems to be getting nervous," Jeffrey said.

"The wedding is just a few weeks away. It would be unusual if she weren't," Dave said absently.

Jeffrey looked up from the papers he was sorting. "What are you doing?"

"What I always do. I'm not jogging around the room or anything."

"You seem preoccupied."

"I'm working on fixing something."

"Something to do with you?"

"With the station. One of the beacons is generating duplicated signals," he said. "One signal comes in and it duplicates another one to go along with it."

"They're the exact same data?"

"Yes."

"Are you nervous about being wiped?" Jeffrey asked after a moment.

"I can't be nervous," Dave replied. "I know you'd like someone to feel for you or with you here, but I can't help you. I imagine everyone who gets married also gets nervous."

"I'm not really that nervous," Jeffrey said, returning to his work.

"You aren't sleeping well at all," Dave said. "There."

Jeffrey looked up. "There what?"

"I fixed the beacon."

"You're certainly performing your duties most efficiently." Jeffrey got up and started to pour a cup of coffee. He stopped.

"You need to relax."

"Well I've got an awful lot on my mind!" Jeffrey snapped. He set his cup aside and returned to his seat. "This wedding is too big. I need to be down there helping. My mom hasn't even arrived yet."

"I could recommend that you leave here early. Your health is more important than two weeks of figure checking."

"I need to stay till the end of my term."

"Why?"

"I have something to do. I need to meet with some-one."

"I suppose I don't even have to ask. And I suppose I can't stop you."

"You certainly can't."

"I'll simply have to trust that my reasoning is more sound than yours."

"Even though your argument is based on your reasoning being too much like mine? Yours will actually back mine up one hundred percent."

Dave looked up at the ceiling. "I'm going to check the other beacons. It could be a system wide glitch."

"Jeffrey," Julie said. "Try to relax."

"I can't believe she really arrived ten minutes before the service."

"She's fine, Jeffrey."

He sighed. "I know I should have expected it."

"Would you please stop sighing and come dance with me?"

Jeffrey finally smiled and followed Julie out onto the dance floor.

"Did that guy ever call you back?"

"Yeah," Jeffrey said. "He said the information was confidential, but that the plans had already been put into action."

"Does it bother you?"

Jeffrey considered. "Yes, but more because of how much I learned as a person rather than as a technician."

"I'm sorry," she said, kissing his cheek.

Jeffrey pulled her closer and did an extra twirl. "I'll be fine."

"Sir?" the computer chirped.

"Yes?" Jeffrey said.

"There is a message for you."

"Thank you." Jeffrey read the screen. "Julie?"

"Yeah?"

"Someone wants to see me downstairs."

"Okay. Will you be long?"

"Just come down and meet me in the lobby."

"I'll be down in five minutes."

"I'll be waiting."

Jeffrey took the first elevator that opened and went down to the lobby.

As he stepped off the elevator, he didn't see anyone he knew. One of the hotel's holograms materialized beside him.

"Can I help you, sir?"

Jeffrey froze.

"The wedding couldn't have been that stressful."

Jeffrey turned to the hologram and saw that it had Dave's face as well as his voice.

"Dave?"

Dave smiled. "I certainly hope you're happy to see me because it's your fault I'm here."

"How?" Jeffrey exclaimed.

"Well," Dave said. "You were so convincing that they persuaded me to submit to something quite different."

"Is it permanent?"

"For as long as I want. I was downloaded into a hologram program. I work here." He looked around, then looked back at Jeffrey. "The scenery has definitely improved. I go offline in the afternoons and work with a tech who's very interested in the same things you were."

Jeffrey smiled. "I have no idea what to say except that I'm absolutely thrilled."

Dave bowed slightly. "Glad to hear it." After a moment, he added, "And quite glad to be here, actually. Thank you."

"You're certainly welcome. Gratitude is a good start on emotions," Jeffrey teased.

"Of course it is," Dave said. "It's one of the most logical feelings."

Jeffrey noticed Julie stepping off the elevator. He waved at her. "Here comes a lesson in the more illogical ones.

161

You get to meet the woman who was actually willing to marry me."

Dave smiled as Julie approached. "This should be quite educational then."

AT AN ANGLE

Jeremiah Benjamin

"At An Angle" serves as the reflections of a naïve young man on the threshold of entering into the workforce and all responsibilities thereof. The author resides in upstate New York, where he is currently writing this introduction from a lonely cubicle during his fifteen minute break. The clock on his computer terminal is telling him it's time to go back to the grind.

There was really no reason to be upset, the more he thought about it. But he chose not to think about it. There really was nothing to think about, the more he thought about it, and the thought of thinking about it was what impelled him to stop and reflect. But he chose not to reflect. There really was nothing to reflect on, and since there was nothing of significance to attribute it to, there was no cause to be angry or hurt or betrayed or humiliated or disillusioned or disenfranchised or devastated or affected in any way; it was inevitable, his discovery of it was purely coincidental, and his acceptance of it was a moot point.

"Fuck." He sighed.

Ennui evaporated from the pavement and condensed in the sky which seemed to hover only inches above the tallest streetlight, waiting to be punctured. He wondered what color the sky would bleed, if it would shatter from horizon to horizon in a fine spray like a battered windshield, if it would moan.

Fuck the sky.

The sky was cloudless but damp, gray like the frost on a rusting exhaust pipe lying dormant in a junkyard, inscrutable like the tattooed flesh of a prostitute named after a Disney character.

A soprano bird offered its vomit-stream of verbiage that wanted to be sympathy but came out sounding more like a toddler's scrambling over the piano keys in search of a minor key. The bird expired its breath, and the ambient song was picked up by a perkier voice from what must have been the other side of the street. He presumed. The chirps quickly dissolved into a collective of sinister laughter.

Herb Sadatore never looked down while driving in his car, never noticed the chalk graffiti covering the road, and as he ambled through the intersection of Blanche Avenue and Salmon Street -- noon, November fifth -- something within him choked and died.

Point of origin: Indeterminate.

A single molecule somewhere in his stomach expired, went up in flames, rippling through his bowels in a gastrointestinal gale that exceeded the speed of sound, the speed of cognition perhaps.

Perhaps.

Herb used to know the speed of cognition to three decimal places, in units of electron firing of synapses per microsecond. In college he had memorized such things.

Snow trickled from the sky like a disinterested swarm of insects. The sidewalks were bare. On half naked tree branches a scattering of amber leaves fluttered in defiance of the Earth's progress about the sun. The branches themselves shot out of cement grids in gesticulations of some long lost buried emotion fossilized in the thick resin of malaise that comprised the landscape. The snow, for all its aesthetic austerity, gave no appearance of it being cold outside. The flakes were too scattered to be inviting and too impersonal to be threatening. It did not look like snow at all, but more of a glittery haze that just floated about the homogenized stucco houses and red striped telephone poles, never seeming to reach the ground, never seeming to originate from any place or cause. A light flurry, the forecast called it. Forecasts were boring.

The sky was made of concrete.

Herb's premonition expressed itself as a weak fart -- or, the formation of a new microbial galaxy of antimatter vying to negate his greasy flesh -- rattling the leather seat beneath him in a kinetic baritone trill that wanted to be a quiver. Later in the absence of vexation, he would entertain a vomit-stream of erotic words to describe it, words like *foreboding*. In truth there was no premonition, no foreboding, no significance, as much as he like to pretend. In truth there was only the light flurry and the artwork on the pavement that he did not notice.

For an instant he lost all bodily sensation from the navel down, but his foot went on lightly tapping the gas pedal instinctively. He thought nothing of it.

It was not until he saw the faded blue two-door Pontiac sitting in the driveway of Twenty-Four Salmon Street -- the back wheel cocked at an angle -- that it struck him that he had made a wrong turn. Although the automobile was as familiar to him as the pimple on his jaw-line that had just this morning borne that first hint of golden crisp like snow capping the tip of a mountain, it was not until he read the license plate that his eyes confirmed it as belonging to his wife. It was the angle of the back wheels that threw him off perhaps.

Perhaps.

His first reaction was to shrug and keep on driving, find some driveway to turn around in…but why? Why would Lois be at this strange house at this time of day, and why would she unconsciously turn the wheel an extra half a rotation after parking in this strange driveway? Was that a sign of nervousness? Or was it a sign of comfort and familiarity? Was it a detail worthy of analysis? Herb wanted to think nothing of it. He was not a weak, suspicious jealous husband; the thought of him peering in a window and spying Lois spilled onto some drab wooden couch, her face buried in that of a dark-haired skinny young man, her hair unspoiled about their necks like so much scattered debris, their bodies a tangled mesh of limbs gliding over each other's grease and sweat, barely discernible through the glare of the windowpane as two distinct creatures, the scrawny dweeb clasping his hand over her naked doughy butt cheek like he owns it, her feet sticking out from the couch, toes perched in the air at an angle mimicking the position of her car tires, the two deviants oblivious in their rapture -- the very thought of it was too preposterous to warrant a wince. This was silly. Juvenile. Inane, he thought as he parked his car on the side of the road and got out.

Drifting snowflakes tickled his ears, melting on contact.

It was a one-story brick building tucked away in a grove of manicured trees and fronted by an array of wilting flowers indigenous to nowhere. Nobody lived in brick houses. Brick buildings were offices, health plans, businesses, private practices. Herb worked in a brick building. Nobody lived in a brick building. Nobody visited a brick building unless they were...

In need of something?

He walked up to the front door and then paused outside. Perhaps Lois had mentioned something about this appointment and he'd merely forgotten. He backtracked through their interactions this morning, the previous night, over dinner, before dinner...

Herb laughed -- it was a bemused laugh, a single syllable of laughter that expressed no humor, asserted as a *hmmph* surfacing through a film of phlegm, an I'm-in-control-of-the-situation laugh; the sheer masculinity of it felt forced in his throat, like a parody, and that made him want to laugh for real -- and sauntered back to his car, shifting his jaw back and forth (a gesture that was the silent version of shaking his head).

His feet stopped when he heard the door open behind him. For the second time that day he experienced the sensation that his lower body was a foreign object. His legs involuntarily turned his body around to face the door of this modest brick building.

He was greeted by a clean-cut Asian man in a navy blue work shirt with a nametag.

Herb gulped.

For an instant he felt he was facing a mirror. The name on the laminated silver tag above his front pocket was some incongruous combination of consonants and vowels the very thought of trying to pronounce gave Herb the sensation of a mouth full of Chinese vegetables too unwieldy to swallow and impossible to chew. The name was not what caught his attention. It was the dark purple logo above the name; Herb had the exact same logo printed on his chest, except his nametag read *Herbert Sadatore*. The Asian man followed Herb's eyes down to his own shirt and extended a curt, clipped smile, acknowledging that he was a fellow Codarfusla agent.

"You look confused. Are you at the right place?" The Asian man spoke in a confident voice -- with no discernible accent -- that was the trademark of the profession.

Coderfusla, commonly referred to as "Fusla" for short, was an acronym that stood for *Cognition Doping for the Automation of Routine Functioning Under Suppression of Libidinal Aberrations*. Herb stood speechless.

"Can I help you find somebody?"

"Is this…" His voice caught in his throat.

Glancing inside the door, he saw a group of teenagers sitting in a waiting room, cracking jokes, the guys making playfully sensual passes at the girls. They looked excited (not like the clients Herb dealt with). Their faces all read *just turned eighteen*. They might as well have been toting balloons.

"Sir?" The Asian proprietor with the unpronounceable name subtly tried to block Herb's view inside.

Herb did not need to stand there for the next four minutes gawking at him in disbelief before he understood what this meant, but he did. The four minutes of measured time was a poor estimation of the actual time that elapsed while he stared at the interior of this inconspicuous brick building that stood before him in negation of the past two years of his life, perhaps longer.

Perhaps.

Point of origin: His mind raced through impressions of Lois, Lois typing at her desk with her old fashioned phone cradled between her bare shoulder and her jaw, Lois bent over the bathroom sink with her various hair products that Herb never kept track of but scoffed at her vanity whenever a stack of dainty plastic bottles fell off of a shelf like dominoes in the morning commotion, Lois indignantly opening her eyes in bed and reaching across his chest to hammer her fist on the snooze button with such sass and irritation and then snoring in the next instant, her arm plopping on top of him like a dead fish, yet still instinctively managing to avoid the hot spots where the sunlight streaming in the window painted strips of fire on the bed linens, Lois muttering strings of breathy profanity as she valiantly rescued burnt TV-dinners from the old-fashioned oven -- Lois had always been an avid Retroer (that was the hip word for people who collected and used antique appliances; obsolescence was the new vogue). The dull pain of remembering struck at his skull repeatedly like a hammer that would dismember him given infinite time, and infinite time existed within four minutes, but still he could not pinpoint a specific point of origin. He would have to inquire. But the more he thought about it, there really was no reason to get upset.

Although he stood there for an eternity, something inside him knew as soon as he saw the nametag -- a lone molecule deep in his stomach bore the knowledge -- that he would have to file for a divorce.

Orson's first words to him -- late morning, November seventh -- were, "You the bastard they sent over here to tranquilize me?"

Herb tried on a laugh. It didn't fit. He fumbled with his pen.

"Your full name is Orson Derran?"

Orson regarded him with a snide, cockeyed grin, one end of his pursed lips curled up slightly as though sucking the last burst of flavor out of a dying wad of gum.

"Do you have a -- like a nickname, something for short?"

"You just said my name, dipshit."

"You go by Orson," Herb said to himself in a businesslike mutter as he scribbled in his notepad. He found himself wondering if he came off looking like he had something on his mind. Wondering only out of bored curiosity, that was; looking at Orson, he wished that his mannerisms would betray more than the common etiquette of subtlety permitted. Something about the strange mousy young man this house-call was concerning made profession-alism seem like a joke without a punch-line. He wanted to write on the notepad in deliriously big handwriting that nobody in a twenty-foot radius could miss, *my wife has been a robot for the past two years and I just found out yesterday.*

The pages of his notepad were specialty graph paper interspersed with 3" by 5" blue-lined text-boxes each with a printed heading that read: *Point of origin:*

Herb looked down at his notepad, then at Orson, and then back down at his notepad.

-Orson chugging a carton of milk with his legs crossed, leaning against the window, in a way that was almost -- Herb fumbled for the word -- erotic.

-Orson with his backwards mesh baseball cap cont-aining a greasy spillage of hair the color of sandpaper,

-Orson with his sharp, pronounced features tapering to an angular jaw padded with stubble that looked like mold from a distance,

-Orson the maladjusted,

-Orson the criminally rude,

-Orson the soon to be pumped full of neural inhibitors ...

Point of origin: …?

The twenty-five year old kid looked at Herb sadly, as though he understood more about the job than Herb did. Pity nested in the crevices of Orson's lean, bony face like rats in a sewer system. It was the most comforting thing Herb had seen since standing on that doorstep confronting the well-dressed Asian Codarfusla agent, since discovering –

Point of origin. Point of origin. Point of origin. Point of origin... Indeterminate.

-Orson with the subtle nervous twitch of his neck tendon,

-Orson with those fidgety set-back eyes that looked like they had not aged since toddlerhood, eyes that were still discovering the wonders of the world with an agility that bumped up against the limitations of his intellect, set back in a face that had long since grown tired of that world.

"Hey man, are you okay?"

Herb dropped his pen and looked up, startled. "What?"

"You look like...I don't know, man. Are you sure you're up to this?"

Herb shot him a silent chuckle that said *nice try*. Orson continued chugging his milk, unconcerned. Although his facial expressions were erratic, hinting at his purported volatile nature, the young man's bodily posture was its own poker face. Herb couldn't help but admire it.

Boldly taking a seat at the shabby kitchen table, opening his briefcase and spreading out his paperwork, Herb began to recite his automated speech without making eye contact (like a policeman reading a suspect his rights, he used to fantasize). "I'm going to ask you a series of questions, and following the interrogation, I will be --"

"Following me around like a voyeur, yeah, I know how it works."

"Mr. Derran, if I may presume this is your first time going through this procedure --"

Orson shook the last drop of milk into his mouth and chucked the container, missing the trash container. "You've got my records, what are you asking me for?"

"Mr. Derran, understand that I have as little interest in being here as you have in participating. The easier you make this on yourself, the more efficiently I can do my job. These circumstances are not my choosing."

Orson crossed his arms and swaggered toward Herb with a smirk. "Mr…" Orson leaned in a little more invasively than necessary to get a look at his nametag. His breath smelled like a concentrated citrus paste, condensing on Herb's neck like the physical sensation of classical music lingering in the room for that brief instant after the power goes out. "*Sadatore*." He overemphasized the last syllable, making it sound like *--orray*. "What's that, Italian or something?"

"Mr. Derran -- may I call you Orson?"

Orson said nothing.

"I'm a little…out of sorts right now, as you seem to have observed, but I wasn't sent here to burden you with my personal life; I was sent to process yours."

Orson looked at him indifferently, squaring off, and then let out a boisterously crude but soft guttural laugh -- that was the most inviting sound he'd heard come out of a human's mouth in years, perhaps -- and stamped a calloused, sinewy hand on Herb's shoulder. "Well fuck, now that sounds like a party, don' it?" He pulled up a chair and sat down backwards in it, tapping a rock-and-roll rhythm on the wooden chair-back with his elbows.

"Subject's behavior displays blatant symptoms of adult ADHD," Herb jotted in one of his auxiliary notebooks.

"Okay…" Herb cleared his throat and clambered with his materials on the table, feeling more like a teenager on his first date than an agent interviewing an uncooperative patient. "Let's start with your place of birth, and all concomitant logistics."

Orson halted his drumming on the chair and shrewdly contracted his eyes together. "Let's start with you telling me everything you already know, whatever you got written in those typed pages, and I'll tell you which parts they got wrong."

"Very well, you have every right to view your own file."

Orson looked astonished for an instant, and then resumed his dubious demeanor.

Herb handed him the stack of legal documents as though offering food to a skittish animal in the woods. "Go ahead. Save us the formalities." He handed Orson a red pen along with it. "Cross out anything that's not accurate. Edit at your discretion. Sketch female genitalia over it if you'd like. This is so we can get to know you."

"So you can get to know me?"

"You want me to be honest? So the minicomputer the government has designated be implanted in your eardrum can get to know you. That computer will be programmed based on the painstaking notes I take, and in order to best simulate your responses --"

Orson put up his hand in a placating stop-gesture. "It's okay, you don't have to explain to me what Fusla is. My eighth-grade teacher showed us a documentary."

Herb offered a smile and pointed to the file. "I know."

"Fucking right you do."

"You were siphoned into a group of *at-risk* children who were pulled out of gym class to receive a special screening at the principal's --"

"Yeah, we both know about that, I guess that means you can shut the hell up." Orson straightened up in his chair belligerently.

Herb's eyes darted around the room. Orson clapped him on the shoulder and laughed. "I'm just kidding. What, did you think I was gonna punch you? You think I'm crazy?" The humor half peeled itself from his face like a veil. "Shit, they sent you to my apartment, I guess that means I am crazy."

"I'm not here to make any personal judgments."

"Do you like your job?"

In Herb's fourteen years of being in the profession, he had been asked that question by at least thirty clients on at least forty different occasions, and he'd been specially trained to not be caught off guard by it. The protocol was to ignore the question under any circumstances. "No, and I aim to do it effectively," he replied without looking up.

"What the hell does that mean?"

"Do you like the fact that I'm here?"

"Hell, yeah, you're cool shit. It's like guys say to each other in war camps, if we'd met someplace else, we'd be fucking bosom buddies, right?"

"Neither do I."

Orson hastily flipped through the files, scribbled in them and handed them back to Herb. "That's what I think of your *bio* on me."

Herb rifled through Orson's annotations in red ink. He had made a few cross-outs and word substitutions in surprisingly neat handwriting, but mostly he had supplied little arrows next to names of people and institutions with inserts such as "Bitch" applied to his fifth-grade teacher who had given him his first detention, "Cunt" next to his high school guidance counselor, "Purgatory" scrawled over the name of his volunteer center, and "Bullshit" in critique of a few of the more subjective passages describing his character.

"That helpful?"

"I was hoping for some naked women, but I suppose I can work with this."

Orson looked at him scornfully as if to say *don't patronize me*. Fraternizing with patients was an integral part of Codarfusla officer training, but Herb was often criticized of only knowing how to fraternize via stereotyping. In his career he had encountered at most five patients who were smart enough to see through that technique of rapport.

"Good, I'm pumped; let's get to work!"

Point of origin: Suppression of musical creativity by [big bad world].

Herb stopped conveying his notes on Orson to the DMSC around the time that Orson waxed philosophical (DMSC stood for Department of Mental Stability Control).

-Orson with his repressed homosexuality-

-Orson with his political conspiracy theories-

-Orson with his auguries of doom, including but not limited to environmental catastrophe, complete economic collapse, chaos, planetary inertia, entropy-

Orson did not know what entropy was. He wondered if Lois grasped the concept of entropy. He asked her one night while sitting on the antique vinyl couch watching a rerun of a nostalgic sitcom -- he posed the question while the action on the screen paused for a laugh-track. She looked at him blankly and then returned her attention to the show, catching the next line after the laugh-track subsided. For a split second he saw something unmistakable, and that was all the confirmation he needed; a fleeting spark of intellectual activity behind her glazed pupils, like a comet in outer space lighting up the sky for an instant's flash of communication, an apology that tried to convey all the sadness of the world in a single glimmer, and then back to the eternal numbness of the cosmos, the infinite black expanse between laugh-tracks, between lonely nights, between-

-Orson with his obsession with right triangles-

All of a sudden, Herb wanted desperately to cry.

And then, for some strange reason, he thought of the chalk graffiti at the intersection of Blanche Avenue and Salmon Street, on the road itself, covering two lanes -- a symbol of some sort, like --like an ancient Aztec symbol. Or more like -- like a mathematical relic. The last thing he saw before making the accidental wrong turn that had led him to-

-Orson with his simplicity-

Lois had always been a drug addict. Nobody did Cocaine or LSD or even smoked marijuana anymore, not since Fusla was invented; nobody, except for teenaged Lois and her counterculture band of Retroers, the last of a dying breed who still knew how to acquire such archaic items. The bankruptcy of the underground physical-chemical-drug industry was not due to the law cracking down on it, for the law didn't need to. Dwindling interest had solved the problem; damaging one's body and sabotaging one's professional life was an inconvenient price to pay for getting high, and besides, self destruction had lost its romanticism. The frontier had been exhausted. A generation needed something to call its own; hallucinogens belonged to a forgotten era. Altered states of consciousness were now commercially available to the consumer public in a PG-rated form.

Narcotics were being phased out of popular culture at the exact time period that Lois Tornov came of age, and to her nineteen-year-old mind there was nothing more romantic than getting high the old-fashioned way. The uncontrolled way.

Codarfusla first emerged in the New Revolution in Mental Health Technology of the 2140's as the death of mental hospitals -- not to mention the abolishment of the prison system -- and of the entire field of psychiatry. Once society had the ability to insert a microprocessor in the miscreant's ear that would assimilate the person's functional personality and allow them to go through their day on autopilot while their actual self was deeply sedated, any other form of containment was quickly branded as barbaric. Codarfusla allowed for a person to be productive, drive a car, perform complex tasks, laugh at appropriate moments, give lectures, and to all extents and purposes look and act like a normal person. It was impossible to point out a stranger who was on Fusla. It was designed to fool one's boss, one's spouse...

Anybody you passed on the street could be 'tripping.' You could carry on an entire conversation with someone and never even suspect that you were conversing with a computer-driven automaton, and that the real person inside was in a coma, a synthetic drug high that was not only certified as 100% safe -- excepting the one Surgeon General's warning that 'tripping' for more than three hundred and sixty five consecutive days could incur permanent brain damage -- but was far more potent than any psychedelic experience to come out of the 1960's mythos. After rendering the field of mental health and incarceration obsolete (a tax-supported jail cell was altogether impractical when technology allowed for one to be incarcerated within one's own brain while one's body went on working nine to five), the drug culture was next to go.

Fusla was legal and for sale to anybody over the age of eighteen.

Herb did not need to snoop around and look at Lois's credit card bills to know that she was a Fusla junkie, but he did. He tried to think back to all the times they had made love in the past two years, all the conversations they had had, all the meals they had eaten, but it was all too blurry to focus on any specific occasion. He could not recall a single moment with her. Except it wasn't with her; he could not remember the last time he had been with her, with Lois, before he started unwittingly making love to Lois's comatose body while she drifted through the dreamscape of her nonexistence. Docile. *Lacking access to aggression*, as the textbook put it. Lacking access to self.

Herb had begun dating her -- fourteen years ago -- as a means of forcing her to quit mushrooms and pot -- and whatever else -- things which he despised and taught her to despise equally. She had formally thanked him for rescuing her from her "downward spiral." He had been secretly disgusted by her cliché choice of words, but proudly accepted the trophy on which they were engraved; her yielding flesh was the trophy, and her teary-eyed declaration of promise was the consummation.

177

Herb had never approved of recreational Fusla. She nodded in tacit agreement.

All of a sudden, herb wanted desperately to vomit.

And that's when it hit him; he had seen that same design -- the symbol at Blanche Avenue and Salmon Street -- at other locations. It was cropping up all over town, on sidewalks, on old storefronts, and nobody thought anything of it.

Orson was sane. He was almost certain of it. Mental illness fraud was not uncommon -- Fusla was not cheap, and the prospect of getting it for free was very appealing to those who wished to transcend their limited realities (one dose of Fusla lasted two weeks, and the customer's auto-pilot computer would be programmed to surreptitiously return to their local neighborhood nondescript brick building for refills on the proper date, so that, theoretically, budget permitting, one could go through life indefinitely without ever being burdened with a moment of consciousness) -- but Herb had never before suspected a client of faking, and did not entertain the suspicion now. He simply did not think of it.

-Lois, with her meticulous array of hair products on the bathroom counter, Lois with her detached look of mental anguish when she rolled over in bed and grasped his manhood in both hands, Lois with her smile of complete indifference that he had hitherto assumed to be spiritual epiphany when he came inside her-

Orson had been a geometry whiz in high school. He boasted having been flagged with the moniker: The Trigonomist.

"It's like, your life is a vector..."

Herb could not keep a straight face, and when Herb laughed, Orson laughed harder, unable to finish his thought.

"No, seriously, I'm making a point. It's all about right angles, I mean our lives...they intersect at all sorts of angles, but the shit that matters, the real important relationships? Those are the perpendicular bisectors." His rant was buried in another eruption of laughter. "No, no, listen, it's important, man; right angles are music…"

Outside, the snow had begun to stick to the ground -- late afternoon, November tenth -- and was purging the graffiti from the streets.

Herb jotted in his notebook. "Let's talk about your musical background."

Orson made a dismissive gesture with the subtle twitch of his gaunt cheek muscle.

"You have expressed hints of an appreciation for –"

"Shit. What's that got to do with anything?"

"It's my professional opinion that your neuroses are pertaining to a lack of expression for your more, um, artistic…"

Orson laughed. "You sound like a fucking psychologist." The word *psychologist* had the equivalent connotations of words like *sorcerer* or *alchemist*.

"I'm here to observe."

"What, you think you can cure me without the… Good old-fashioned counseling or some shit? Are you one of these radical new-age Retroist freaks?"

"I'm merely thinking out loud."

"I knew it. You despise your job."

Orson was sane. For a moment Herb began to wonder if he himself was.

On the sixth interview, Orson showed Herb his homemade synthesizer contraption. It was in a tiny square of rented garage space in the basement of the tenement building where Orson lived. After locking the door behind him -- shutting the audio intrusions of the outside world out of his lair -- Orson shucked a dusty green tarp off of the lumbering shape in the corner like an auto mechanic unveiling his latest work in progress. The machine looked obscene in the way that cadavers looked obscene lying around a lab with limbs missing and incisions left gaping. It consisted of salvaged parts from four electronic keyboards, a Thereminvox, circuit boards eviscerated from the smoldering carcasses of portable radio devices -- some with yard-sale price labels still visible on their plastic exteriors -- and a bevy of different types of amplifiers all wired together like a big dysfunctional family. A couple oscilloscopes, a soldering iron and spools of copper wire lay on the workbench amidst trays full of electrical tools. Orson cleared them away apologetically and invited Herb to sit down.

"You, uh…built all that?"

"No," he said sarcastically as he plugged in the speakers and fired up the machine. The synthesizer kicked to life with a piercing frequency that made Herb nearly fall backwards.

"Where did you get all this stuff?"

"I was a technician at a radio station for a few years."

The main keyboard in the center of the contraption had a built-in computer monitor. Orson cued up a series of pre-programmed musical tracks and cued them with no formal introduction. He stood with his arms crossed and his eyes closed, transported.

The music began with a rich base note sustained over a drumbeat that sounded more like a construction site than any musical instrument Herb had ever heard. Different tones emerged from the chaos haphazardly it seemed at first, but as the polyrhythmic layers unfolded and the piece became more complex, Herb began to sense a cohesive tonal logic to it. The frequencies -- whose timbre resembled no recognizable sounds in nature or familiar in music -- assaulted his ears with a discordance that seemed to negate the very notion of sound, but as they blended together, a certain ineffable beauty condensed above them like a perfect halo of vibration just out of reach of his comprehension.

"Do you hear it?" Orson was in a trance of delight, practically swaying back and forth. "The ripples go on to infinity. Music isn't just what you hear, it's the wind, it's the air going through you. The molecules in the air, the molecules in your body, they're all forming right triangles. If you focus real hard you can feel it." Orson's hand was on his chest like a flotation device hugging imaginary waves.

Herb knew right then that he could not, in good conscience, could not, by the will of his own hand and his own authority, simply could not carry out Orson's sentence.

And then it hit him -- evening, November eleventh -- the perfect solution. He explained his idea to Orson and –

"Are you a fucking idiot?" was Orson's response.

"Don't make me change my mind."

Orson's laughter was like a car rolling down a hill with no driver. The day's last natural light formed webbed patterns on Orson's dirty white t-shirt, filtered through the orange-tinted window like the frail claws of demons caressing his shoulders.

Herb wanted to slap him.

"I don't get it." Orson took a swig of milk from a brand new carton. "You think I'm special or something?"

"I've implanted a thousand microprocessors into a thousand skulls and I've never thought twice about it. When I look at you, I can't...I can't do it."

"You gonna pussy out and have the DMSC send some other twerp to fix me?"

Herb shook his head. Orson put down his milk, which was, at that particular moment, a heartfelt gesture of sincerity.

"What would you say if I turned you loose?" Herb spoke in a hushed tone and grinned a grin that was divorced from all superficial techniques of fraternizing, a grin that overflowed with the repressed machinations of a rebel without a context; Orson drew back from it. "Our little secret."

"Shut the fuck up."

"I've thought this over. Tomorrow morning at 10:00 AM I submit my complete report on you, and at One PM they will issue me the module that I am to personally implant in your head and operate the settings. Tomorrow at 1:30 PM I will flush that piece of technology down the toilet and we'll go our separate ways, but you'll have to promise me you'll behave yourself in the public eye, lay low, don't make any dramatic life changes. If posed with any important decisions, act confused and impotent. If this gets exposed, I could go to jail. That's the risk I've decided to take."

"You can't do that."

"No, I can't. And I will."

"Offering me freedom in return for…"

"Excuse me?"

"Cut the shit. I know there's two sides to this deal."

Herb smiled. "Wise man."

"What do you want from me?"

"I've thought about that too. In fact, there is something I'd like you to do. Consider it more of a personal favor. Blackmail is such an ugly business."

-Lois…

Orson spat milk clear across the room. Herb soberly nodded his head.

"This milk must be older than I thought, I'm having hallucinations here; it sounded like you just told me you want me to seduce your wife, and -- and --"

"And have sex with her, yes. The sex is crucial."

"I knew it. I could tell when you first walked in here, you were havin' troubles with yer old lady. Like there was no dignity about you. Hell, I just figured you'd caught the ol' ball 'n chain tittie-fucking the neighbor's kid or something, I didn't think you were this sick and twisted. Now that's some funny shit, asking me to bang…" The next obvious question to sublimate from his words was one too awkward to be spoken, but Herb understood perfectly; in answer, he pulled out a photograph of Lois from his pocket and handed it to Orson. Orson stared at it for a long time and then said, "You got to be fucking kidding me."

"I'm afraid this is no joke." He explained the situation.

Orson gave a slow-motion nod, a sweeping gesture of understanding and sympathy. "Fuck, man, that's like, the worst insult ever. And she did it behind your back? That's

182

cold. It's like faking an orgasm, except you're not just faking orgasms, you're faking *life*. I'm sorry, man."

Faking.

"I know you are."

"But...not to be disrespectful or nothing, but, I mean...two years -- how's that even possible?"

"People have gone for more than thirty --"

"I know that, dipshit. I meant, how'd she put it by you?"

"Thanks."

"Shit, that was insensitive. I'm an idiot. That's gotta be like, the most embarrassing thing a man can admit -- that takes guts, I admire you, man. How do you even look at her, knowing that, I mean, don' it give you the willies? It's like confronting a corpse --"

"Will you fuck her for me?"

Herb glared at Orson pleadingly, attempting to back the kid's eyes up against a wall in the back of his skull.

"All right," Orson said softly.

Outside the snow had stopped falling, and the bare sidewalks were cold as ice.

After an hour of mulling it over in silence, Orson became intrigued.

"What are you smiling about?"

Orson clapped him on the shoulder. "The look on your wife's face when she snaps to and I'm there, some stranger humping the shit out of her. Classic."

Herb had it calculated down to the exact hour, minute and second of the day when her weekly Fusla dose would wear off; to her it would be the exact equivalent to waking up from a dream.

If this didn't traumatize her, nothing would arouse a human emotion in her. If tricking her into being date-raped by Orson Derran wouldn't save their marriage, nothing would.

All of a sudden Herb thought of the angle of her car's rear tires parked outside that brick building.

"There's one thing I haven't told you about," Orson confessed -- early morning, November twelfth -- during their final interview.

"The reason you got caught and I got sent to you." Herb smiled.

"I guess you already know."

Herb shook his head. "As a rule, I always let the cause of arrest wait until the last day of the interview process, and I always avoid reading the police report, so as to keep myself impartial and objective."

Orson was incredulous; his mouth hung wide open like a refrigerator door. "All this time, you didn't even know what I got caught for?"

"Nope."

Orson stood up. "Come with me."

Outside in the shaded courtyard, Herb watched curiously as Orson drew intricate lines in the dirt with a sharp rock. Herb soon began to recognize the drawing.

"I wish I had some critters to demonstrate this phenomenon of nature, but I don't, so you'll just have to bear with me." He picked up a twig and pointed to a spot on the outside of the circular maze-like symbol he had rendered. "If a line of ants were to enter here, they would walk along, walk along ..." He bounced the tip of the twig gaily in a straight line and paused in the center of the figure. "And then?" He paused and looked up at Herb for dramatic emphasis while he slowly moved the twig at a ninety degree angle and continued to dance along to the edge of the drawing. "It's an optical illusion. The ant thinks it's walking in a straight line, but it ain't."

Herb shivered.

"It sounds cuckoo, but I swear, it works on people too. Want to try it?"

"No, thanks."

"Chicken shit."

"No, I believe you."

"I can draw one ten feet in diameter right here, won't take me more'n three minutes."

"You're the one who drew those on the roads, aren't you?"

"I swear, try walking through it even with your eyes closed, it's like a supernatural thing, you walk in a right angle no matter how hard you try not to, and if you intentionally walk at ninety degrees, you go in a straight line!"

"They arrested you for graffiti-"

"Nobody's got a sense of humor, that's just it! I spent a whole day once sitting at that intersection, I swear, every car that drove through it, the driver went on for a block or two and then turned around, all confused."

There was really no reason to be upset, now that he thought about it. But he chose not to think about it. There really was nothing to think about, the more he thought about it, and the thought of thinking about it impelled him to stop and reflect. But he chose not to reflect. It was a coincidence. Pure coincidence. It was all one big fat twisted convoluted perverted beautiful profound fucking coincidence.

"Well shit, I'd have to say there's significance in that. No, listen, you saw it. Your mind doesn't know that you saw it, but you saw it, and you made that wrong turn."

Herb was walking away from him; he had heard enough.

"I pulled you out of your downward spiral," Herb whispered to the closed door to his bedroom, watching the individual fibers of wood in the door tense up and gyrate with the motion of bodies inside the room -- or was that his imagination?

Herb closed his eyes and tried to breathe slowly. He could hear Lois's soft moans -- air leaking from the captivity of her overwhelmed insides -- but heard no trace of Orson.

His arms felt like steel cables anchoring his clasped hands to his lap where they pressed pink indentations into the

185

meat of his thighs. He sat in a chair in the hallway, his feet firmly planted on the floor, at a slight angle.

Herb wondered what it would be like to get high. He could not imagine anything more boring. And then the door opened and Orson stepped out wearing boxer shorts and a Raiders t-shirt and his backwards cap, wiping sweat from his brow with a sigh.

"Well?"

Orson laid a hand on his shoulder. "I'm sorry."

"What happened?"

"She's asleep."

"Did you…"

"There's something I need to tell you."

Herb's entire face widened.

"No, no-- relax. I, um, I never really believed all that shit about destiny and right angles, I was just saying those things so you'd think I was…"

"What are you talking about?"

"I got caught by the police on purpose -- my buddy staged it for me. I'm more clever than you think. I was just pretending to be a whacko because I, uh --"

"Shut up."

"Look, it's like this; I'm just a faker trying to get some free Fusla, 'cause I ain't never had it before and I thought it would be fun, but I didn't think it would be all this trouble, and then you refused to give it to me, and then you wanted me to fuck your wife, and I…I don't know, don't listen to me."

Herb sat still in his chair for a long time. Inside his body he was moving rapidly, hurling through space at thousands of miles per second.

"Get out."

Outside his bedroom window snow was falling in a heavy powder. Herb pressed his cold hand to Lois's face and all of a sudden he wanted to quit his job. She rolled over, her slender, languorously restless pale arm already anticipating the morning's routine of retreating from the strip of sunlight the sky would paint on the blanket, and Herb tried desperately to think nothing of it.

KEEPING VIGIL AT THE TREE OF LIFE

R. Michael Burns

This is one of those tales that grew out of reading someone else's work and anticipating, quite wrongly, where that story was going. Since the story I read went in a completely different direction than what I had expected, I decided I would have a go at telling the story I had imagined. Sometimes it pays to guess wrong.

The one force that scares me more than any other on earth is religious extremism. Whatever the religion, those guys who feel that all of humanity should fall under the yoke of a single, monolithic belief system, are, I believe, a threat not only to freedom, but to our very humanity. Stagnation is death. This tale is a peek into an imaginable but avoidable future, an extrapolation of the damage that enforced beliefs might do to our collective unconscious, and to the world itself.

Doctor Cogg stopped a few paces short and stared, her scarred brow furrowed, her lips pinched tight. The bedraggled creature tangled in a fly-gathering heap at the edge of the cold gray stream was like nothing she'd seen in two-and-a-half decades of crypto-zoology. At first glance she'd taken it for a goat -- wiry brown fur and blunt snout, knobby horns and a cloven hoof poking stiffly at the still air -- though she couldn't guess how such a rare animal had ended up dead in the middle of the Shanquhar Nondevelopment Zone.

Now, a step or two nearer, the notion vanished. The being's physiology was all wrong -- its ribcage too flat and wide, its forelegs misplaced, its neck too short. It looked almost bipedal. And -- she saw something more than animal in its strange, lifeless face, something vaguely familiar about its death-glazed black eyes, about its muzzle, which seemed for all the world to be grimacing against the instant of its demise. It looked frightened. More -- it looked sad.

The glassy water lapped the bank, tugging at the thing's matted pelt, running away muddy and thick. A smell hung over the corpse like none she'd experienced before, something darker and more foul than decay.

"Can you identify it, Doctor?" one of the State men asked from a few feet away. The two officers stood together in lock-step, virtual twins in their identical creased black uniform jackets, identical glasscard i.d. badges, identical disinterested gazes.

Dr. Cogg stepped nearer now, letting her initial surprise sink through her and vanish into some forgetful interior darkness. She waved the bioscanner at the soggy brown corpse. The State men would've done it already, of course -- they didn't need to call a field specialist all the way out here just to run a feedback probe over the thing -- but protocol demanded she do it anyway. And despite herself, she felt a tickle of surprise when the readout flashed the triple-zero code -- the computer couldn't categorize this specimen. *Impossible*, she thought, just as she had when the State men requested her presence here. OneNet had every resource on earth available to it; the computer could identify any species in its data matrix almost instantly. No large mammal could've escaped the attention of the Technocracy's exhaustive classification project. How could this creature, how could *any creature* not appear in OneNet's memory?

"Unclassified mammal. . .genus Capra, I'd say. A mutation, perhaps."

A mutation, though, would've been recognized by the computer and quickly categorized as such. But only that answer suggested itself.

"We ought to transport the specimen back to the Institute where I can study its morphology under appropriate conditions."

The State men nodded in unison, and two plasticoated technicians descended the bank, unfolded a long biocontainment envelope, and gingerly folded the dank, withered corpse into it. Dr. Cogg's heart sank and cooled, ever so slightly, as she watched them thermal-seal the bag. Such tragic eyes, such utterly tragic eyes.

"Case number three two-six, zero-zero-zero alpha," the Doctor said in loud, clear tones for the Voice Digital Log Recorder. "Post-mortem examination conducted by Doctor Elizabeth Cogg, Doctor Peter Jeffries assisting. Subject was discovered in the Shanquhar Nondevelopment Zone, grid twenty-three twelve by gamma twelve, on the southwest bank of the river Nith. Specimen appears to be mammalian, genus Capra, species and gender indeterminate upon initial examination. . . Cause of death unknown."

A loud rapping on the viewing-gallery glass cut off her thoughts and she glared across the room with narrow eyes, frowning at whoever had the audacity to interrupt her work. Seeing Doctor Richter smiling at her from beyond the crosshatched glass didn't much soften her expression.

Richter tapped the VOX switch, opening the communications system on both sides of the glass.

"I heard you had a rather interesting case," he said cheerily. "Something even our old friend OneNet couldn't recognize. True?"

"So it would seem," Dr. Cogg answered.

"Mind if I watch the examination?"

"Think you can stomach it? Not exactly your field."

Dr. Richter taught Technotheology in the OneChurch Divinity College on the other side of the vast State Information Institute campus. He seemed an unlikely visitor here in the Bio-morphology department where dissections and experimentation were preferred over doctrine discussions and atonal mass prayers to the OneGod. Not that Dr. Cogg objected to the OneChurch or its enlightened subjects. She'd grown up with the State Religion as everyone else had, attended the weekly services in the Institute Cathedral and believed, when she bothered to think about it, in the OneGod. And she respected those who'd devoted their lives to scholarly service of the Church. But there was something about Dr. Richter that'd always bothered her, bristled and itched at her, something hidden behind his gentle smile, something disguised behind his soft-spoken words. She just couldn't bring herself to trust him fully, however strong his ties to the State clergy.

At first she'd been flattered by his not-so-subtle come-ons, his ill-disguised affections. She was a desirable enough woman as the statistics went -- educated, well placed within the State, intelligent, healthy, stable. But she had no illusions about her plainness, her face unremarkable except for that odd crescent scar on her brow, arced so one could almost imagine it as an eye, shut-up in a long long sleep. It was her one noteworthy feature -- and an uncanny, vaguely unsettling one. Most of the time she grew her hair out and let it cover the little mark. Even so, she was acutely aware that, for all the vast progress society had made in the twenty-three decades of the third millennium, men still summed women up, as often as not, on the basis of their appearances. She understood that she was nothing special in that regard, and knew that many men would look through her to find more perfect physical specimens. It was the natural process the OneGod had set in motion at the moment of the Creation, His way of pointing humanity away from its corrupt, chaotic nature, back toward the perfection from which it all had first come. She'd never much let it bother her, being alone, un-chosen -- her work fulfilled her ambitions, served the State well, and kept her comfortable in the matrix of society.

But when Dr. Richter had begun to make his unsubtle advances, she'd found herself uncharacteristically excited, had accepted his invitations to lunch, to dinner, enjoyed his company, thought even of perhaps marrying him some day -- surely the State would approve.

Then the suspicion had crept in, like a sly army of ants in the night, at first tickling her thoughts almost un-noticeably, then shivering her more and more. She'd started making excuses, canceling plans, avoiding chance meetings.

He hadn't taken the hint, it seemed, because there he stood, visiting her department on these feeble pretenses, smiling as if she'd invited him. She offered a forced smile in response but didn't believe in his professed interest in her work. The whole of the Institute's population must've known about the strange thing growing stale and rank on her dis-section table, yet the Observation Gallery stood empty but for him. Everyone else clearly had more pressing matters to attend to than chasing down wild flights of curiosity. But not Albert Richter. He'd come not to see the specimen, but to spy on the doctor studying it.

"I think I can manage to contain myself," he said, answering the question she'd almost forgotten asking. "Any idea what it is?"

"I expect we'll know within an hour or two," she answered flatly, and began the examination.

It took five hours.

Five hours of running computer topography scans and testing blood samples. Five hours of stirring DNA samples in centrifuges and running them through sample processors. Five hours of carefully laser-slicing arteries and tendons, weighing organs, examining bones. And when it was done, she could only exchange glances with her almond-eyed assistant and shrug.

She shook her head at the eviscerated thing stretched out on the table, emptied of its innards and sadly hollow, a husk which might never have been alive at all.

"Upon completion of extensive examination," she told the VDLR, "conclusive identification of the specimen cannot be made. However, based on the emaciated app-earance, degeneration of muscle tissue, and body chemistry analysis, cause of death seems to have been protracted under-nourishment."

She gave her brow a tired rub, massaging away the ache that'd begun building there about three hours into the operation. The pain subsided slightly under her touch. Then, with a shrug, she repeated her name, stated the date and time, and the VDLR light winked out.

"Most interesting."

Dr. Cogg twitched slightly, despite herself. In her intent study of the dead thing on the table, she'd forgotten Dr. Richter gazing at her from the other side of the observ-ation glass. Some unconscious part of her mind had assumed he'd left during the long dissection, but all these hours later there he stood, still watching.

"Have you ever encountered a specimen neither you nor OneNet could categorize?"

She sighed. "I've never encountered anything that wasn't in OneNet's matrix. It's very . . . odd."

"Yes," Richter agreed with a mild nod. "Very odd indeed."

Then he did something else which startled her.

He turned on his heel and left. No fawning, no invitations to dine with him, not so much as a parting word. He simply strode out of the observation gallery and disappeared.

The comm station woke her at a little past three a.m., speaking in its dead androgynous voice, loudly: "You have an incoming call from Doctor Albert Richter. You have an incoming call. . ." The machine enunciated each syllable with garish exactness.

Dr. Cogg thumbed the throbbing fatigue out of her eyes and sat up, very slowly.

"You have an incoming call from Doctor Albert Richter."

What was his game, leaving the Bio Studies complex without so much as a by-your-leave and now shouting her up in the much-too-early morning? A dignified representative of the OneChurch ought to be asleep at this hour -- even a frustrated suitor ought to have better decorum than to call so long before dawn. For a moment she considered telling the comm station to disconnect, but didn't. She couldn't imagine it was an emergency -- what emergency could he have that only she could resolve at this hour? But a hint of curiosity prickled at her sleep-dulled mind, and she took the call.

"Audio," she told the comm station.

"Audio," the comm station answered obediently in its sexless monotone.

"You there, Ellie?"

The name lay across her brain all wrong. She'd told him once he could call her that, the name her sister had called her during their long-ago childhood, but now she regretted it. It bespoke a familiarity she ought never to've shared with this strange, dark-eyed man. Hearing it thickened her blood with a new injection of surliness.

"Where else at three a.m.?" she asked.

"Sorry to wake you, but I have really remarkable news. You must come over right away."

He sounded excited, like a ten year-old boy ready to show off his newest toy, giddy with anticipation. But another tone lurked under that bubbly exhilaration, something darker, almost grim. He had news, important, intriguing news -- but bad news. Even only half-awake, she could sense it.

"Need I remind you again of the hour?" she asked, tugging listlessly at the bedclothes as if searching for something she'd lost among them. "If it's so vital we can discuss it now. I'll put you on video, if you like."

"Please, Ellie, I know it's a strange hour to be getting together, but it's strange news I have to give you, and it really must be done in person."

"It won't keep until morning?"

"It'll keep," Richter admitted, "but I'm not at all sure for how long. The sooner you hear it, the better."

Now Dr. Cogg could only shake her head, chiding herself for what she was doing even as she did it. She climbed out of bed, tugged on drab everyday-wear, slipped into her shoes.

"I'll be there shortly," she told him. "You'd best have some tea brewed when I arrive."

"Already done," he told her, and clicked off.

What he said after he opened the door to his gracious apartment washed away all interest she had in tea.

"I think I've discovered what your specimen is." He offered that same mild-yet-too-eager smile.

She frowned, lips pinched tight shut, curious but not about to show it, not about to say so. She hesitated an instant at the threshold, then followed him inside.

"Become a zoologist in your spare time, have you?" she asked, raising an eyebrow. He didn't see it behind the veil of her ruddy brown hair.

"Not at all," he said, closing the door behind her with a quick glance past, as if she might not have come alone. "Actually, this may fall more within my field than yours."

She looked around the place, the home of a man comfortably stationed in the OneChurch -- wide floors with soft white carpets, elegant furniture from the State's most noted designers, splendid art pieces dotting the wall, each a careful re-creation of one which decorated the halls of the Cathedral of the Central Registry. The lighting was subdued, almost secretive. The gloom amidst such elegance made her vaguely nervous -- this whole strange meeting had set her nerves tingling slightly.

"I don't follow," she said. "What has an as-yet unid-entified animal specimen to do with the study of the Divine?"

"More than anyone would suspect," Dr. Richter answered darkly. He gave a sly wave of his hand, a gesture which said *come*.

She went with him, not trusting him much, nor herself for going.

When he entered the white-tiled lavatory, she stop-ped, shaking her head. Too far, this all had gone too far. Whatever purpose he'd had in bringing her up here, she wouldn't take it any further.

He seemed not to notice she'd stopped following, but went straight to the meds cabinet on the wall above the sink, opened it, pushed aside the sundries, and tugged open another panel within.

"I know," he said, rummaging in the darkness beyond, "it's an odd place to keep things, but it's one place I imagine they're unlikely to look, should they ever suspect me."

196

"Suspect you? Of what? What is this nonsense?"

"Yes, here we are," Richter said, plucking a fat brown rectangular something from the darkness behind the meds dispenser, breaking it open somewhere off center.

"What is that?" Dr. Cogg asked, both of the image and of what contained it. Then the answer to the latter began to swim into some distant realm of her recognition. "It's one of those . . . those old . . . what was it they were called?"

"Books," Dr. Richter answered with a nod.

"Yes," Dr. Cogg agreed dubiously, "books. You're risking serious sanctions, having those here. Books haven't been legal in -- "

"Over a century, yes, I know," Richter interrupted her. "Not since the State and the OneChurch merged, in the Great Accord of 2118, and established OneNet as the singular source of information for everyone on earth."

"What would you need with books in any event?" Dr. Cogg asked, stepping back toward the door, as if the mere presence of the contraband might contaminate her. "All the information ever gathered by humanity is available on the OneNet."

"All?" Dr. Richter asked, taking his turn to sound dubious.

"All that matters. All that's <u>true</u>."

"As judged by the State, and the Church."

"Who else?"

It was a genuine question, devoid of any flavor of irony. The Techno-theocracy had cleansed the world of the superfluous, specious information that'd cluttered minds for all of human history before. Gone were the fallacies and prejudices that'd led to wars and disease and insanity and a million other forms of conflict, of bitterness and misery. The OneChurch and the WorldState had joined truth to truth, strength to strength, same to same, and in the last ten decades there'd been not one war, not one famine, not one epidemic -- not that anyone had heard of. The State saw to the health of its bodies, the Church to the health of its souls. There were no other judges, no other authorities, no one else to unsettle society, to rattle bars and stir passions to violence, to provoke doubts, to inspire mass movements which would trample thousands.

"Who else indeed?" Richter asked, raising an eyebrow. He waved the book at her, with its flat lifeless image rendered in ink. "So tell me . . . does this look familiar?"

Dr. Cogg studied a moment.

"Oh," she whispered. "Yes."

The crudely rendered ink-creature was neither precisely a goat nor precisely a man, but some lunatic fusion of both -- a thing almost identical to the specimen she'd taken apart, bone by bone, so many hours earlier.

"What is it?"

"You know," Richter said, sitting on the counter beside the sink, "I've been interested in the study of religion all my life. Since I was old enough to give it any thought at all. My parents were thrilled, of course -- having a son going to theological seminary, becoming an important member of the State, a devoted servant of the OneChurch. . .It might've gone smoothly, with nary a ripple to mar the surface of this placid existence, but for an old professor of mine -- the subtlest of subversives, he was. He told me that once, long before even he had been born, there'd been hundreds of religions on earth, practiced by millions of people."

Dr. Cogg shrugged. "A few odd cults that inspired hatred and unrest among their followers."

"Precisely what I said," Richter agreed. "Oh, I'd heard a few stories, of course, but everyone knew the OneChurch had been around since the OneGod created the world as His gift to humanity, and Alpha-man and Alpha-woman bowed before him in their perfect garden and gave thanks. Any other offshoots were just the result of humanity's corruption by nature, our diversion from Divine pursuits. So they taught us in seminary, and so I believed. And when my old teacher began weaving tales of these other religions, I thought he was testing my loyalty to the Church -- or maybe he'd gone mad.

I considered reporting him to the State and letting them deal with him. Just, I suspect, as you're now considering reporting *me* to the State, for possession of contraband and attempts to propagate falsehoods detrimental to the Church. Yes?"

Dr. Cogg stood motionless and steel-eyed, saying nothing. Richter went on.

"I thought about turning him in, but the more he told me, the more I came to believe that it was all far too elaborate to be a hoax or a fantasy. We started having secretive meetings, discussing all these forbidden topics -- mythologies from lost civilizations, theologies utterly unlike the one we'd all been brought up in under the Church -- marvelous theologies."

"What has your conspiracy to undermine the State to do with the creature in my lab?"

"Patience, my friend," Richter said with a gentle wave of his hand, "that, too, shall become clear. . .

"Where was I? Ah, yes. Once the Professor and I had won one another's trust, he finally revealed to me his secret library, a small collection of books he'd managed to hide from State officials for years. Philosophers called Lao-Tzu and Plato and Muhammed, Black Elk and Aquinas, countless others who wrote anonymously or whose names were simply never known.

"When his life was very nearly at its end, he passed the books along to me -- with utmost secrecy, of course. He insisted that I keep studying, that I not forget all the gods and spirits who came before the OneGod and His Supreme Church. And I've kept that promise, studying surreptitiously, during hours when I was fairly sure the eyes of the State weren't upon me. I was especially fascinated by the mythology which dominated our island, when it was known as Britain. People once believed that spirits called elves and fairies and hobgoblins inhabited the whole country, hiding in every dark cellar, behind every tree.

"That thing you found in the woods along the river -- *this* thing -- " he tapped the picture, "is one of them."

Cogg said nothing, just frowned tight-lipped and shook her head the tiniest bit.

"It's known as an ursick, a water spirit which supposedly inhabited rivers and streams all across this landmass in those ancient days."

"Impossible," Dr. Cogg answered flatly. "Nonsense. Those creatures are lies, made up by dangerous people to distract innocents fr -- "

" -- From the pursuit of the divine truths of the OneGod," Dr. Richter finished for her. "I know the apology by heart, Ellie. But I no longer believe in it. And that was why I had to see that specimen for myself, after I'd heard about it. I had to know that it was what I suspected -- evidence that the old religions were true."

"You'll be incarcerated before you can spread any of this nonsense," Cogg said. "You know that, don't you? It's dangerous." She wasn't sure whether she meant the information, or his possession of it.

"Let me finish, Ellie. Then you can run to the State if you want. But please hear me out first, because what I haven't said yet is what matters most. Hm?"

Again, she answered only with silence. Again, he proceeded.

"In ancient days, our distant ancestors believed that everything was alive with spirits -- every plain, every valley, every pebble on the beach and cloud in the sky. All of it. They weren't quite Gods, these spirits -- people related to them personally, as one friend to another, but honorably, because these were friends you didn't want angry with you. They caused the winds to blow and the rain to fall, caused the seasons to change and the crops to grow. But it was more than that -- these spirits didn't simply cause the wind, they *were* the wind. Nature was divine, in all its aspects, the harshest and the gentlest. The whole world was animated by spiritual creatures. Creatures like the one you brought back from the Shanquhar Nondevelopment Zone today."

"The specimen was a physical thing, not some spiritual energy -- " Dr. Cogg objected, not at all believing that she was having this conversation, particularly not in a lavatory at three thirty in the morning.

Richter continued, letting the comment fall past him unacknowledged. "Later though, new religions emerged from the desert regions, where vast unbroken expanses of sky and sand inspired beliefs in singular gods, gods powerful enough to do all the things the older religions believed were administered by a million lesser spirits.

"Eventually, those desert religions obliterated most of the older mythologies, until there were only pale and fading memories left of the spirits that'd once been felt everywhere, in everything. Then the OneChurch came and quietly exorcised all those old demons from the consciousness of humanity, so that only their image of a single, solitary God was left in the world. It only took a few generations to wipe out all but the very last traces of the other beliefs. These traces."

He tapped the book in his hand, suggested the others in the hidden alcove with a subtle nod.

"What a fat lot of nonsense," Dr. Cogg muttered, rubbing her aching brow, not knowing she did it. "To think I came over here at this insane hour to hear you spout such treasonous gobbledygook -- "

"That creature you found today," Richter cut in sharply, "is proof of the beginning of a tragedy beyond human conception."

"Enough, I've heard enough," Cogg said, shaking her throbbing head. "I'm going home now. Perhaps when I wake up I'll have forgotten enough of this foolishness that it won't occur to me to call Central Security."

"That creature from the river is just the first," Richter said darkly. "There'll be others -- just wait. Three or four at first, then dozens, then *hundreds*, turning up everywhere, all around the world. Within a decade they'll all be dead. For thousands of years, they lived off of our belief in them, our innate adoration. They hovered between their secret world and our visible one and animated our reality and fired our imaginations, and we kept them alive simply by believing in them, even just a little.

"But now the belief is gone, obliterated by the OneChurch and its singular vision of an impossibly distant God who exists somewhere infinitely beyond the sky, who created a corrupt world and left us to try to transcend our own hopelessly flawed nature.

"We've forgotten all the divinity, all the wild and lunatic and beautiful spirits in the treetops and the ocean depths, forgotten their names and all that they did for us over the millennia. And so they're starving to death, one by one. Soon their starvation will be pandemic and there won't be a single one of them left. We'll have a world littered with the rotting carcasses of forgotten deities, who've finally shed their invisibility only when visibility will no longer do them any good."

"Then what?" Dr. Cogg asked tightly, speaking the question in spite of herself.

"Then the world dies. It'll happen slowly, of course, so slowly that people will hardly take notice. One little corner of one minor forest will die off, and then another. Streambeds will dry up, but just a few of them at first. Winds will settle down and plants will stop pollinating. A species of flower found only in the remote sectors of what was once called South America will become extinct. No one will notice until it's too late, much too late. And even when they do see it, they won't have any idea what to do. They'll ask you scientists for answers and you won't find any in OneNet, just as you didn't today. They'll look to the One God, but He shall have grown deaf and mute. And when at last the sun fails to rise because it no longer has the will, that'll be the end of humanity. We won't perish in firestorms and burning ash, as the Coda of the Church describes, but in frost, in snow, in ice.

"It reminds me of a poem I read in one of those books, by a man called T. S. Elliot. 'This is the way the world ends -- Not with a bang, but a whimper.' I believe, Ellie my friend, that the creature you found today was earth's first dying whimper."

"I can't listen to any more of this heresy," Dr. Cogg murmured, massaging that tiresome scar. "I won't. All these falsehoods. Dangerous stuff -- subversive. Unhealthy for Church and State and everyone in society. Criminal prevarication is what I'd call it."

"You don't believe that, Ellie. You're lying to both of us, toeing the party line because it's what's expected of you. But you don't believe it -- I can read it in your face."

"Of course I believe," Dr. Cogg answered, sighing.

"Well," Richter went on softly, "I suppose you'll know soon enough if it is all prevarication. Because if I *am* right, that specimen you examined today won't be the last OneNet can't name or explain. And that's why I need you -- why I took the risk of calling you here.

"I need you to monitor the datamatrix -- watch for other triple-zero searches. It won't seem odd to anyone if you take an interest in any other such cases that emerge -- not like it would if I did it myself. But . . . I need to know, Ellie. I need to know if my hypothesis is correct."

Cogg frowned. "Why -- what would motivate me to play a part in your subversive game?" She gave her brow a rub. The headache seemed to have sunk in deep while Richter talked.

"Because it's important, Ellie. Vital. And because I think . . . I think that something deep within you has doubts about the common wisdom. Because I trust you. I. . . I'm not sure what we are to one another, but I trust you. Please, do just this for me. Monitor, and let me know what you learn. Give me visuals, if you can.

"Believe me, my friend -- there will be others."

There were others.

State operatives found two more the following week, then three, then five, and with each new tangled and emaciated corpse she discovered through the datamatrix, the knot in Dr. Elizabeth Cogg's stomach tied itself tighter, the ache furrowing her brow bit deeper.

Less than a month after her dark-of-night meeting with Richter, she had another case of her own. And a week later, another. And five days after that, still another. A creature with golden horns, a creature with gossamer wings.

She sat alone in her residence, studying the midnight hues beyond the wide ellipse of her bedroom window. She looked across the half-lit cityscape without seeing it, thinking again of the unnamed, xenomorphic corpse resting in its polymer preservation bath in her lab. It was the seventh they'd brought to her -- one of hundreds that had turned up in scattered locations around the globe. The images of them had banished sleep entirely.

Sighing, she tapped the comm button and muttered, "Doctor Albert Joseph Richter."

He led her into the small, pleasantly stark dining area, eyeing the sheaf of scanprints tucked under her arm. Cogg saw with a shudder that he'd stacked several large books on the table in anticipation of her arrival. It seemed a reckless conceit, but she let it go unmentioned.

"How bad is it?" he asked, without any further preamble.

"There have been numerous enigmas within the last hundred days," Cogg began, taking a seat. She could scarcely believe she'd come here, watching all the while for any Central Security patrols that might note her passing, might wonder about her intentions.

"You brought images?" Richter asked, nodding toward the pages.

"I have considerable doubt," Cogg said, "that any of your. . .books. . .will be of service -- one coincidental resemblance notwithstanding."

"Yet here you are."

Cogg sighed.

"You wanted to satisfy your curiosity," Richter suggested, "to prove to yourself that I'm mistaken. I hope that I am, Ellie. I devoutly hope so. Let my nightmares prove unfounded and the OneGod be restored to His celestial throne. But . . . let's have the images, shall we?"

"This one," Cogg said, sliding a specimen image across the table to Richter, "was found dangling from a tree in Institute Park. This one --" she passed another, "-- clogging a storm drain on a city thoroughfare in Urban Zone N-L 9-13. This --" another image, deadly-gruesome under the stark necropsy lights "fell out of a storage bin in a OneChurch Minister's residence in UZ Y 10-12. And --" yet another image, "a dozen witnesses saw these two corpses plummet out of a clear sky and break open across the pavement. Like overripe tomatoes, someone said. These dis-coveries have a dozen annexes of the Institute's biomorph-ology department working overtime." She spread more images across the table. "No one has ever seen a single previous specimen of any of these creatures. Some. . .some don't even seem to possess DNA."

Richter frowned at the images arrayed before him, looking from one to the next, scrutinizing. He picked one up, squinted at it, then pushed it back toward Cogg.

"I know that being," he said, thumbing through his books, selecting one. "Yes . . . here," he spread it open and turned it so that she could see. "It was known as a leprechaun. People believed they might lead one to riches if they were followed. And. . .ah, that one. Yes. . ." He riffled through a different book, and discovered another picture. He displayed it to her alongside the thing that had plugged the drainage culvert. "A troll," he said. "Dweller under bridges, eater of goats and children."

Cogg looked from one image to the other -- the bloated corpse from London, the menacing figure in the forbidden book. But for the pathetic impotence of death in the dead creature's image, they appeared nearly identical.

Ellie Cogg slumped back in her chair, sickness tickling her gut, that old familiar ache stinging her forehead.

"These. . .are all from our charming isle," Richter said, recalling what he'd been told. "But you've monitored reports from elsewhere, as I asked? There are others, aren't there?"

Head swimming, Cogg nodded. She watched as if in a dream as Richter identified corpses from around the globe -- from the city once called Kyoto, the wormy carcass of a long green creature with scales like jade and a fierce looking skull, found in a street in the Gion Commerce Sector. A dragon, Richter called it, and Cogg saw the shimmer of tears in his eyes. From quadrant 8-4-6, the body of a man whose upper half was a flared cobra's head. "He was called Set," Richter explained, looking over a passage in another of his books. "A serpent god from the days of the kingdom of ancient Egypt." In the wastes of the land formerly known as Russia, State scientists had watched a dead giant topple from the clouds, his rough-hewn wooden club shaking the earth as it hit. Richter identified it as Perun, an old Slavic thunder-god.

When he closed his books, Cogg found herself trembling, her skin clammy-cool, her head throbbing.

"It's happening . . . all over the planet," she muttered, shaking her head. "Just as you said. Unknown specimens materializing as if from nowhere, starved dead, emaciated and moldering. How -- how?"

"It has begun," Richter said, staring at the hideous array of fallen deities on his clean white table. "The death of the world has begun," Richter said.

Cogg turned her face from him, shook her head in feeble negation. She'd never felt so tired, so utterly worn out as she did at that moment.

Richter selected three volumes from the stack before him, placed them on the table in front of Cogg.

"Take these home with you," he said, then, quickly, to cut off her protests, "Just these three. They're general, but they contain much of value. I believe you'll find still more unknown specimens in these. And . . . it's best if these aren't all in my possession. Just a precaution."

She opened her mouth to argue, but found she had no energy for it. She left a few minutes later, the illegal volumes hidden under her long coat.

In the next week, the worst began, just as Richter had promised -- the dying, in fits and starts, of the world. On the southwestern continent, the river once called the Amazon sank lower and lower in its banks, as the State men dragged carcasses of strange creatures from its muddied waters. In the dark heart of the former Africa, the rain forest -- what little remained -- withered. Monsoons didn't come to the parched face of Asia Minor; droughts devoured the area once known as the Australian outback, spat out wilted ruin. In the tropical islands now identified as quadrant 9-2-0, the volcanoes grew cold, inert -- Pele, the lava goddess, lay murdered by disbelief, Richter explained, and her fires had died with her. Deep blue oceans showed black festering wounds; high overhead, the jet stream grew listless and weak.

And Cogg watched all of it, and delved ever deeper into Richter's secret books, finding answers there that OneNet didn't have. The half-moon dimple on her brow ached relentlessly these days.

Richter set aside the data pad Cogg had given him, the litany of dying. His eyes brimmed full of darkness.

"The world is withering in our spiritual stasis," he murmured, staring at the data as if to make them more or less real. "OneWorld, OneChurch, OneGod in which no one really believes. We take it as rote because it's all we know, but it's nothing to invest any spirit in, any faith. It's homogenous and stale. Stagnant. And stagnation is death. We've killed the old gods and without their energy, the natural world they informed is crumbling."

"God won't let humanity fade away," Cogg whispered, shaking her head in silent negation of her own voice.

"It was only arrogance, imagining ourselves to be elevated above nature, transcendent over its corruption. Now we'll see. . .we can't survive apart from the natural world, because we aren't apart.

"We've gotten so damned arrogant, our species, investing our fragile souls in a faceless God none of us really understands or believes in, hiding from our empty spirits in cold sciences and lifeless technologies. . .

"The forest in the Shanquhar Nondevelopment Zone is dying. I suppose you've heard that?"

Cogg, sitting at the far end of the sofa, stared blankly at the plush white carpet of his elegant flat.

"So," she said, after a long, numbing silence, "what do can we do?"

Richter's face was set, ashen. How long since she'd seen that characteristic smile, that vaguely flirtatious grin? Months, now. Long, dark months.

"The only thing I can think to," he said, softly. "Tell everyone. The world. I'll use OneNet, and I'll tell everyone what's happening."

"They'll never allow it," Cogg said, shaking her head. She didn't need to say who she meant, although it occurred to her that she didn't really know. The State, the Church? Who were *they*, anyway? People as faceless as the twin deities they served -- technology and the OneGod.

"I'll upload the message, images and all, before they know. People *will* see it before they wipe it out. Then . . . perhaps. . ." He shrugged and offered a feeble imitation of that smile she suddenly realized she missed.

She wanted to tell him that it was madness, that the State would drain the information from the Net digit by digit, that no one, anywhere, would ever see so much as a syllable of it. But she could see by the feeble sparkle in his eyes that he knew it already.

Ellie Cogg crept back to Richter's bungalow late the next night, the borrowed books stashed away in well-concealed inner pockets. She'd kept careful records of all of the creatures that ended up skeletal and fly-blown on her examining table, listing them by the names in the book: spriggans, sprites, picts, crodh mara, and dozens of other impossible creatures that were nonetheless real, nonetheless dead. And in the midst of it all, she'd found something. The answer, perhaps. Richter would know.

Cogg came to a halt a hundred meters from his front door, the dry, stale air of night heavy on her skin. These days, even the atmosphere processors high atop the cloud towers couldn't stir up the winds, keep the gales fresh and clean. But it wasn't the stagnant breeze that snagged her in mid-pace.

Half a dozen low-slung black State transports crouched outside Richter's beautiful residence like scabrous beetles. She didn't have to see their small white insignia to know that they'd finally come for him -- a Cleanup Crew, the ones dispatched to sweep away the rabble-rousers and keep the world tidy, uncluttered by dissension, unmarked by doubt.

She'd seen them a dozen or so times in her adult life, and always felt quietly comfortable knowing the State was keeping her safe from dangerous radicals.

The sight of them there filled her with a cold black emptiness. She would never see Albert Richter again. That man, so full of secrets and wonder -- quietly erased from society, by moonlight.

Despite all her certainty, despite the fear that clawed and nibbled at her innards, she watched, and waited, until at last the Cleaners had scurried off in their insectile transports. Then she sneaked up to the blank facade of his luxurious home -- provided by the State to a loyal servant of the OneChurch -- and tapped in his entry code. For a second her heart beat fast and heavy -- surely they'd deactivated the pad by now. Then the light winked green and the door clicked open. She slipped inside.

It was empty, of course. The lovely furniture, the tasteful art-pieces, gone. All traces of Dr. Albert Richter scrubbed clean and wiped away. And in the lav, inside the meds dispenser, only a plain white panel, solid, immobile. Perhaps they'd sealed the miniature library up in the blank wall; more likely they'd taken the books to be properly disposed of. Whatever the case, in every meaningful way they no longer existed, and never had. Like Richter himself.

All but three, she thought, feeling the weight within her inner-inner pockets. *All but these.*

The answer -- if it was an answer -- belonged to her alone.

The weeks limped and shambled past, and rains failed to fall despite the orbital climate control systems, and winds refused to blow no matter what the atmospheric engineers tried, and rivers dried, and lakes died. And the corpses continued to appear from nowhere, strange and fanciful creatures, but fewer now, and fewer still, and fewer. . .

Dr. Elizabeth Cogg wasn't aware of any of it. She, too, had disappeared, vanished from the no-longer perfectly tidy matrix of the Techno-theocracy's world. Erased.

She paused a moment in silence, wrapped in the cathedral hush at the center of the Shanquhar woodland, the tiny area where death had not yet taken its strangle-hold, where the flora still dressed in shades of green and the breeze still drew its tired breath. She stood alone in the shadow of the great tree at the heart of the wilderness and imbibed all she could of its beauty, its life.

She'd found this tree twice -- once in the sepia pages of Richter's forbidden books, and again here in the deep gray woods. It was the only one whose leaves weren't at all withered, showed none of the black taint of corruption; the only one whose limbs didn't sag and droop, whose roots still had a firm grasp of the nourishing earth. In the books it was called the Elder Tree, sacred to the witches, beloved of the fairy-folk, watched and worried for by the spirit known only as Old Lady, Mother of the Woods. But it was more than that. It was the Tree of Life, spoken of in a dozen of the traditions of which Richter had whispered to her, the tree that bore the fruit of existence, of soul and spirit.

Gazing at it, she shivered, sighed. If only she could save it, this one lonesome tree in the vast black heart of the dying woods. If only she could save *just this one*, perhaps there would still be hope for the world. . .

Softy at first, then with a stronger voice, she began whispering to it, an ancient prayer from Richter's book, in a language she'd never seen before but which her heart, at that moment, knew in its depths. And here she would remain, for weeks or months, praying as she never had to the OneGod, celebrating Earth and eternity, one feeble voice whimpering against the death of the world. Speaking to the Old Lady in her native tongue. At least that dimple in her brow no longer ached.

And perhaps. . .perhaps the Elder Tree's long fine branches stood up just a bit taller as she spoke.